Literotica

Carla Keyne

Contents

JAY THE BUBBLE BUTT CHAV

J ay was well known on the Green End Estate for his shitty attitude, always being in trouble with the police and most of all, his juicy fat bubble arse. He could be spotted hanging around the ends at all hours, and even from the top floor of the block of flats, his globular cheeks could be seen protruding obscenely from his tight grey trackies. When he sped round the block on his bike, his meaty cakes jiggled and vibrated on the seat, inspiring raging hard ons from the lads and blokes watching him fly away, cig in his mouth to drop off to his regulars around the way.

19 years old and standing at 5"10 with smooth olive skin, cropped dark hair with taunting eyes and a slit in his eyebrow, jay was an extremely fuckable scally lad. Paired with his big ripe peach and his lack of any regard towards the rules, he was very popular on the estate ... especially with the boys.

It was something that was never discussed openly amongst the men and the lads in the rough working class neighbourhood, but plenty had had the pleasure of getting up close and nasty with jay behind closed doors, the thing is jay wasn't just a chav boi with a big fat arse, he was a chav boi with a big fat arse that demanded to be fucked by as many cocks as possible, and spunked deep full of as many loads as he could get up that sweet pink fuck hole.

Any where he could get it, and the dirtier the better...

On a blazing afternoon in mid August, Jay was hanging out on the balcony with the lads, hand down his pants, guzzling cans of lager, spitting over the edge and passing around spliffs as usual. As they jostled and joked around over the loud grime music playing from inside the flat, jay, with his plump arse balancing on the railing of the balcony, happened to look over his shoulder at the flats opposite, and caught sight of the fit footy coach who lived there with his bird.

6 ft with a shaved head and a broad chest, he stood at his window shirtless-where he had been stood for who knows how long. He held eye contact with jay, who had adopted a mischievous knowing smirk on his handsome face.

Coach Ryan winked at the drunk chav from across the courtyard of the block of flats, licking his lips as his eyes travelled up and down from jays face to his ample booty, hanging over the railing with a visible wet patch running down the crack of his tight grey cotton Adidas shorts, between his beefy cheeks. He flashed jay a devilish grin, groping his stiffy through his black joggers and winked, beckoning the lusty scally lad over.

Feeling the familiar crave in his sweaty hole, he hopped down from the railing of the balcony.

"Catch u in a bit lads yeah?" As he made his way along the front of the flats, letting out a belch.

"Safe bro." the boys called out, discreetly watching his round bubble bouncing ridiculously in his shorts with every step.

He bounded down the stairs, his hungry hole clenching in excitement at the coach's meat he had just witnessed.

A few moments later her rapped his knuckles on the front window of coach Ryan's flat, around the other side of the building so the lads wouldn't catch sight of him.

The door opened quietly, and the coach appeared, his bright blue eyes sparkling and his rounded pecs dripping with beads of sweat from the scorching heat of the afternoon.

ass.

"Be a good slut and do it properly boi. First u gotta get a good whiff off daddy's cock."

Coach Ryan grinned mischievously.

Jay stared up at the buff footy coach and began to instantly inhale the hot, musky pole throbbing in his face. From the coach's heaving nuts up to the juicy head he moved his face up and down, sniffing all along the way.

"Mmmmff coachhh." he moaned " it smells so fuckin fit - ooh I wanna taste it!"

"How bad pig?" coach Ryan teased slapping his pulsing knob against Jay's eager face "be a good bitch and say please."

"Please daddy, I'm gaggin for it. Pleasee!?"

He whined, pursing his juicy pink lips.

"Good lad. since u asked daddy nicely."

Coach Ryan slid the fat purple head of his cock in between Jay's desperate lips, which wrapped around it in response, as the chav lad began to greedily slurp up the rugged coach's schlong.

Gagging, spitting and slobbering, jay guzzled on the huge cock like the slut he was, twerking his big beautiful arse as he worked the cock.

"Ahhhh fuck yeah baby!" groaned coach Ryan, thrusting his pole deep down Jay's throat. " that's it bitch, show daddy how bad you want his meat inside that juicy fat bubble arse!"

Jay gagged and spluttered, defiantly holding eye contact as he choked on the huge cock, gargling all the way to the swollen balls.

"Fuckin ell' boi, you really are a cockslut aren't you?" Coach Ryan winked stroking jays head as he deepthroated his rock hard dong.

"Mmhmmghh!" jay groaned in agreement, his mouth stuffed with cock, just how he liked it.

"Time to spunk that fat arse of yours baby, would u like that?"

Jay stood up, his spit coated face in front of the coach's.

"Yes daddy." he smirked deliciously.

Climbing onto the sofa with his knees spread, jay leant forwards spreading his basketball cheeks wide for the coach. Coach Ryan gawped at the perfect pink boy pussy before him, begging for spunk between those perfectly rounded melons.

"Time to fill u up slut boi."

Grabbing a handful of the lad's mounds he plunged his pole into the warm wet chute, which reacted by greedily sucking it in deeper.

Jays' eyes rolled back as he took every inch of the coach's huge stiff rod

"Oooohhhh fuckkkk coach!" he salivated, arching his back and beginning to jiggle his arse up and down the pole, creating filthy wet sloppy noises, which chimed in with the coach's hard abbs smacking against his cheeks as he picked up the pace of his fucking.

"Aah yeah baby, that's it - work coach's cock- Come on - I know you want this load!" coach Ryan chuckled as he jiggled the bouncing booty in his big man hands "is that what you want baby? Huh?" wrapping his hand around jay's throat - who was moaning and whimpering uncontrollably.

"That's what I want daddyy!"

Looking at the window, jay could see his mates through a gap in the curtain, still up on the balcony smoking up and drinking Stella. He grinned as he began to shake his huge big bum faster and faster up and down coach Ryan's throbbing meat

"Then be a good bitch..." coach Ryan panted as he hammered away at the chav lads sweaty luscious bouncing cakes

"and fart for coach." he moaned tightening his grip on Jay's throat

Jay looked back at the coach lustrously over his shoulder, who had pulled out and had his meaty cock head pressed against Jay's puckered shitter, he stared in his eyes with a smirk

"Like this daddy?" He moaned, letting rip a loud rasping fart all over coach Ryan's cock

"Ahhhh yeahhhh bitch, that's it, fart for daddy- fuck yeahhh!" coach growled, burying his stiffy back between Jay's slutty chav mounds. Slamming harder and harder into his hole, causing jays to push out more and more juicy farts out of his naughty big booty, vibrating around the coach's cock as he moaned in ecstasy at the lads talking pussy

Gripping his cheeks tight, coach plunged balls deep and blasted an arse full of creamy white spunk deep into Jay's guts. Both men panted and heaved as the hung coach inseminated Jay's greedy bubble. Exchanging sloppy wet kisses, shuddering and moaning, finally they fell into a sweaty pile on the couch, grinning and laughing.

"You'd better get back over there with ur lads." coach Ryan smiled, squeezing jays now scarlet red bum cheek.

"Guess I better had coach." jay winked.

Leading him to the door, coach Ryan gave jay a wet snog and gave the boy's big booty a final spank on his way out.

"Mrs is out every Thursday, you be sure to stop by again baby, you hear?"

Looking back over his shoulder and allowing one more glimpse of the rounded fat arse jiggling away, jay threw the coach a cheeky grin

"Yes daddy."

Moments later jay was back with the lads, who passed a joint on arrival.

"Where u been bro?"

"Just had to go see to some business innit bro." jay smirked, as a foamy cum bubble burst out of his arse and ran down his leg.

THE HAREM

- -

M ina woke surrounded by naked limbs.

Some pale, some golden skinned, all beautiful. A sleepy languor filled her body as she looked around the dimly lit room and a small but satisfied smirk tugged at her full lips. Youths piled on the bed, the floor, each other, resting their heads on lush thighs, soft stomachs and hard chests.

How could she want anything else?

As they reached the age of 18, the age of selection, the most beautiful youths were sent to her and her king. And she reveled in her harem.

Its beauty.

Its debauchery.

Her bare feet echoed against the cool marble floor as she made her way to the throne room, torches fixed high on the walls lit the way down the hall, and seeing her King on the dias being pleasured by two of their concubines only added to the sensual mood she found herself in. Azrael's eyes were darkened with lust when they met hers, his voice rough and husky as he called out to her.

"Mina." His dishevelled hair brushed his broad shoulders and fell onto his brow almost covering his beautiful dark eyes. Regal features and a strong jaw were offset by sinfully full lips. What made his finely sculpted body even more magnetic was his effortless aura of strength and power.

Mina's lips met his in greeting before they moved to his ear, her voice husky as she grew more affected by the debauchery laid before her.

"I wish to watch today."

Having made her request she made her way to the throne and spread her legs over the arm rests, waving a hand in an air befitting a queen expecting obedience.

The male concubine currently worshipping the king's sex was a fey like boy. Dark hair set against alabaster skin, an innocent face and body that begged to be violated. He was a gift from a neighboring kingdom, a virgin sacrifice to barbaric gods given at the perfect selection age.

A ripe fruit waiting to be devoured.

Azrael felt his cock throb at the thought of further corrupting him.

Mina watched on as a darker skinned female concubine cradled the boy into her, pulling his knees up to his chest so that his small pink hole was exposed to the king's hungry gaze.

Mina couldn't stop her hand from wandering down to her leaking folds if she tried.

Azrael watched the boy's back arch as the woman stroked his length, plac-ing the head of his sizable cock at the boy's tight entrance. This seemed to distract the boy slightly and he looked down, his eyes growing wide at the terrifyingly arousing sight.

A snap of her fingers had a strapping young man crawling to the throne and devouring her the wetness that was growing steadily between her thighs, the concubine worshipped her sex as was expected of a subject to his Queen. Mina's eyes were firmly fixed on Azrael's turgid length as he pushed into the squealing boy. Even as he cried out his little cock was rock hard because he was in the presence of the most powerful King in all the realm. He could not stop himself from responding to the King's raw power

His sweet cries filled the room and Mina felt herself grow even wetter. The harem boy between her thighs moaned as he was gifted with more of her nectar to coat his tongue.

The King began to dominate the boy with slow, deep thrusts. His thick shaft forced the boys hole to stretch wide and every time he filled the boy completely he smirked at the guttural moans that escaped his pretty pink lips.

Mina let her hands tangle in the hair of the concubine between her legs, tugging hard as he drove her closer to the edge with his skillful tongue. Between watching her beloved and having her concubine worship her with his mouth she was quickly approaching her peak.

The King himself was starting to fuck the boy faster, no longer teasing but slamming into his tight hole with the sole purpose of filling the boy with his cum. The sounds of pleasure from the throne room started to draw more concubines as they woke one by one. Soon the entire throne room was filled with beautiful concubines of all shapes and shades, and the heady atmosphere grew heavier as the concubines began to join in the debauchery themselves.

As the rest of the castle woke, the usual moans and cries were heard from the many bedrooms, the alcoves hidden in the hallways, and even from the stairwell when a pair of lovers had lost all patience to be joined.

This was the kind of day that made Mina proud to be Queen.

And just like that, surrounded by debauchery and hedonistic delights she felt herself come undone. The concubine between her legs dutifully and eagerly kept tasting her, quickly growing addicted to the unique flavor of his Queen as she cried out- her sweet voice filling the throne room.

At the same time the King roared in triumph as he found his pleasure within the tight depths of the boy, holding his hips bruisingly tight as he buried himself fully in the boys' hole and filled him to the brim with his thick creamy seed.

When the King finally released the boy and stood, the the boy was left in the arms of the lush bodied concubine who'd held him up during his ravagement. His hole was gaping wide and leaking cum down his leg. The boy himself had spilled his seed as the King had pounded away at a spot inside him that had him screaming. So he was covered in his own seed as well, his eyes glazed over and his face flushed from the pleasure he had received with the King's attention.

The King went to his Queen, sitting in his throne beside her and snapping his fingers so that another concubine knelt between his legs and started licking the cum off his thick shaft.

"Did you enjoy yourself my love?" The King asked curiously, an amused smirk on his lips because Mina was still shaking with every lick of the male concubine she felt on her over sensitive sex.

"Very.. very much, beloved." She stammered, taking another moment to enjoy the almost painful pleasure of overstimulation before she pushed the concubine's head away. When he pouted at the loss of the taste of her, she leaned down and kissed him slowly. Finally pulling away the concubine looked as dazed as the new boy on the floor, and just as content.

Mina turned to look at her beloved and held out her hand to him, entwining their fingers when he took her hand and smiling because she knew both of them were far from done in reveling in the debauchery of their kingdom.

The day had only just begun.

CORSET FITTING AT THE RENN FEST 1

Thirty minutes after Lia should have been at Evie's house, Evie called her. "Where are you?" she asked, exasperated, as she eyed the rapidly-moving morning interstate traffic outside her apartment window. "We aren't going to get there to see the opening ceremonies!" Evie had just recently seen an ad on TV for this Renaissance Festival at the local fairgrounds that sounded like a lot of fun, so she and Lia had made plans to go.

A groan answered. "Evie...I met this man last night and..." her friend began.

"Ok, so you got some...so what! This meant a lot to me," Evie complained, disappointed yet again. What was it about sex with men that had Lia so worked up that she forgot all her promises? Sex wasn't that great – just some guy pounding away on top of you, and you having to fake an orgasm at the end. Masturbation...now that was way better. That way, you could fantasize about whomever you wanted, in whatever situation.

Evie was aware she wasn't as good looking as her friend Lia. She and Lia had been friends since middle school, so she was used to being passed over by guys. Evie was truly shy about her looks and she'd learned to hide behind books and glasses, while her friend Lia was more outgoing and social. Lia was model material – medium length black hair, striking green eyes, pert breasts, and she was over 5'7" in height. Evie, on the other hand, was shorter, with what she thought of as a dumpy figure – but she was actually truly curvaceous, with large breasts and a firm, round ass. She was 5'4," petite, with long, curling brown hair and blue eyes. She had a 36D bust, but she had learned to conceal it with body shapers and uncomfortable bras. Why wasn't it still fashionable to have a large bust?

Evie sighed, pulled back into the conversation by her friend Lia's insistent voice. "...Anyway, you just wouldn't believe him. Stamina like a horse, and hung like it too. I think he's a keeper, at least for a little while..." Lia's pause told Evie she should say something.

"Great. Congrats. I guess I'll go to the Renn Faire on my birthday by myself."

"Evie, no, really, I can get ready and be there in like, an hour and a half, I just have to get ready..."

"Forget it, Lia, I'm walking out the door. I know how long you take. We'd be lucky to get there by the time it closes." Evie sighed again, and hung up the phone on her friend. What a way to start a birthday. Lia had a new boy toy and, once again, she had to take the back seat to her friend's passions. Being the friend of a drama major certainly had its drawbacks.

***

As Evie drove up to the wooded fairgrounds, she looked around, appreciating how beautiful the day was. It was early fall, and the air had a crisp bite to it; the sun through the trees fell in long golden bars. She felt a shiver of anticipation, and smiled for the first time that day. "Even though the day may be going bad," she said to herself, "I still feel like I'm going to Disney World." The comparison stuck with her as she watched hundreds of costumed people walk up to the castle-like gates, and as what was presumably a Knight and some Ladies wave down to the crowds. "Hey, I wonder if that's King Arthur," she mused to herself. She felt a sudden stab of disappointment in herself that she couldn't find anything remotely "Medievalish" to wear – she'd had to settle for a t-shirt and blue jeans. Even Lia had planned to dress up. She sighed and got out of her car, walking down the long gravel road to the Faire.

Once Evie was inside the gates, she was greeted by the ticket lady. "How do you do, Milady. Welcome to the Faire."

Evie smiled at the girl, momentarily surprised by the greeting. "T-thanks. You have a beautiful dress." The dress was a maroon velvet, with a lace-up bodice at the top embroidered with wild roses. It was probably one of the most beautiful dresses she'd ever seen. The girl's milky white breasts contrasted sharply with the red velvet, drawing the eyes to their perfect roundness. They heaved and quivered with every breath.

"Thanks!" She smiled at Evie. "It certainly captures the attention, doesn't it? I got it over there at Lacey's Emporium. They know how to fit a Lady."

Evie thanked the girl again, and wandered off into the Faire, program in hand. She was still blushing lightly from the encounter. Why not wear something like that if you could get away with it? The girl certainly looked good in it, and it was a perfect fit. Evie blushed again. What was it about those Renaissance outfits that made her lose her train of thought? She'd never been attracted to other women, not really, except to admire their beauty. She began to doubt her own mind, but she tried to put it out of her head and enjoy all the different sights at the Faire.

***

After walking around the Faire for about two hours, and having consumed a famous Turkey leg and a mug of spiced hot cider, Evie passed by a large crowd watching the jousters. What was it about men and their poles? Or even swordfighting? She giggled, thinking, "The longer the sword, the shorter the..."

The minstrels had almost finished playing, and she paused to listen to a sad ballad about a lost lady love. The music was just amazing – it was like nothing she'd ever listened to. It felt right to be there, the sun on her back and the sound of the lute, guitar, and a lovely harmony. They finished up with a rousing drinking song, "12 Nights Drunk," and she laughed until she almost hiccuped.

"Really?" The woman arched an eyebrow, then she seemed to drop the issue. "My name is Milady Rose deWinter. Our establishment is Lacey's Emporium; we sell custom-made and off-the rack fine garments for the discerning Lady and Lord. How can I assist you today, Milady? I have a beautiful blue velvet cloak that would accent your eyes." Evie looked away from Rose. "I was looking for a bodice for a friend. She was planning on coming with me today, but she couldn't..."

Rose shook her head, one curl tumbling down lower to curl around her left breast. Unaware of the affect she was having on Evie, she said, "I don't recommend buying a bodice without having a professional fit it to someone. It's hard to get an accurate fit, especially the first time."

Evie felt her nipples tighten as she watched Rose's curl tumble down. "Oh, God," she thought, "this woman is driving me insane! And she isn't even doing anything!"

Noting Evie's silence, Rose reached out to her. "Don't worry; we can always find something for you, though. You have the perfect body for Renaissance garb! A velvet or brocade corset, perhaps, one that laces up the front – a white shift underneath, and an overskirt....let me see..." Rose led Evie through the stuffed racks of clothing. Evie noticed all the fantastic, mul-tilayered "Fairie" skirts. Several of the bodices she passed by had beautiful embroidered symbols on them, pentagrams and Celtic knotwork. Finally they were at the back of the store, where there was a small fitting room area with a mirror and numerous, more embroidered dresses and bodices.

"Many I make one-of-a-kind," Rose said, noticing Evie's amazed look at the kaleidoscope of brocade, dazzling crystal, and yards of detailed embroidery.

"You must be proud...you are such an artist," Evie exclaimed, true awe in Rose's ability coming through in her voice.

Rose bent over, carefully moving bodices out of the way. "I'm searching for one particular one," she explained. "Sometimes you just feel when a client is right for a corset."

Evie watched Rose as she bent over the pile of bodices. Rose's corset was drawn tight, but not too tight, accenting her long, almost slender waist and ending at the swell of her hips. Evie could see the rise of Rose's round breasts straining against the top of her low-cut bodice. Her breasts were smaller than Evie's, but not by much. They mounded against the velvet top, pushed together by the fabric and the boning of the corset. A sprinkle of small freckles like stars disappeared down into the small valley between her breasts. Suddenly Evie could think of nothing else other than to reach into Rose's bodice and feel her breasts, suckle on her nipples. Her panties again became wet.

"I found it! I knew it was here somewhere," Rose exclaimed. She straight-ened up, looking at Evie. Evie rapidly tried to compose her face, and look at what Rose had found.

"I could never wear that," Evie said, disappointed. The corset was made completely of a cornflower blue velvet, cut dangerously low in the front, with a small lace modesty panel in the middle. It had large silver eyeholes, lacing up from below the waist to the top of the modesty panel. The corset was covered with detailed white embroidery of snow, shimmering in silver and white. It had no sleeves, only a small drape of blue velvet material to accent the scooped-out, low neckline. It was complete with a long blue velvet skirt made of many panels, like a gypsy skirt, complete with small silver bells. "Maybe you'd prefer to wear this?" Rose smiled, then held up a gauzy belly-dancing outfit. It had a large, gold-embroidered demi-bra, and sheer, completely see-through pants. "Absolutely not!" Evie felt her face get hot from the racy outfit. The ones she'd seen at the performance seemed tame by comparison. "What are those for?"

"Private performances." Rose grinned at her, and Evie thought she was teasing her. "This blue velvet outfit – it's the one I made for the lady who was going to play Morgaine, then she had to back out of the Faire. I think it'd be perfect for you. At least, until you can get something custom-made."

"Ok. I'll try it on – but I don't think I can afford something like this. It must have taken you forever to sew it," Evie said.

"I think we can work something out," Rose glanced over at her, and then turned and led her to the dressing room. It was larger than Evie had expected, with sturdy wooden walls and a large, velvet padded bench facing a full-length mirror. "Wait here a moment." Rose went back to the front of the store, closing the large wooden doors to the entrance. Now everything was shadowy, though some light did come in from the windows at the top. Looking at Evie, Rose said, "I thought you might want some privacy..." She smiled, and held out the bodice and skirt. "You might need these."

Evie hung the bodice and skirt on the wooden peg, closed the curtain across the door, and sat down on the bench. "My God," she thought, "can I even try this?" Her hands were shaking and she was sure her wetness was making a stain on her panties. "Is she as attracted to me as I am to her?"

Something lacy and white came flying over the curtain. "Put these on," Rose called. "After all, your best dress demands good undergarments. And call me before you start trying to lace up that corset!"

Evie stared in shock at an incredibly beautiful sheer white thong, embroidered with a single silver snowflake. Was Rose out of her mind? Evie didn't like thongs that much, anyway, and why did Rose say that she had to lace her up?

"Umm...Rose," she called, "did you just say that you were going to lace my corset up?" Evie felt her blush traveling all the way to the tips of her toes.

Rose pushed aside the curtains, hazel eyes twinkling. "It's the only way to get a true fit, especially the first time. You know. Like a bra fitting."

Evie felt her eyes widen as a pulse of arousal hit her already drenched pussy. "Really?" she whispered, her voice sounding high and childish to her.

"Really," Rose affirmed. "Don't worry; you have a great figure, and I'm the only one here." She closed the curtain firmly. "I promise I'll be gentle."

Evie could only pray she would be.

***

"What's taking you so long?" Evie heard Rose call over the curtain.

convincing to herself. She wished she weren't so attracted to Evie, but she couldn't hide her feelings very well. Maybe she should just get this over with.

"Lean over a bit. Ok." Rose reached in past the velvet, and discovered an even far softer velvet than she ever knew existed. Evie's breasts were silk and velvet beneath her fingertips, and burning hot. A blush that must have started in Evie's cheeks colored her white breasts with a warm sprinkle of color. Rose brushed her fingers against Evie's hardened and apparently aroused nipple, and didn't miss the sudden shiver that rocked Evie's body. She supported Evie's back with her other hand, and gently cupped her breast, finally, with her whole hand. Her fingers wrapped around the whole weight of the breast, like holding a large cantaloupe in one hand. Rose shuddered, feeling the tingle in the palm of her hand spreading through-out her whole body. Quickly, she lifted Evie's breast, and then lifted and adjusted her other breast. Rose was in shock as to how Evie was making her feel. Why did it have to hit her so hard, and so suddenly, with this woman?

CORSET FITTING AT THE RENN FEST 2

Evie almost cried out as a wave of pure lust hit her from the way Rose was touching her. Surely she must feel it too. She almost cried out in desperation as Rose's touch became impersonal, almost rough. Maybe she was just horny; maybe she was just imagining things.

Rose decided that the situation was now or never. Perhaps she was only imagining things with Evie, but she had to know. Finishing the lacing on Evie's corset, she tightened the last lace and tied a bow. Her voice sounded husky, even to herself, as she said, "There. You're all done. But I really don't like that skirt. Why don't you just model in the corset and the panties I gave you." She sat down on the bench, and glanced up at Evie in the mirror.

Evie, facing the mirror, met Rose's eyes. "I think you're right." She tried to be brave, but the words came out as a whisper. "After all, this is my first fitting. And you are the expert." Bending over, she slid the velvet skirt slowly over her hips, letting it pool on the floor. Straightening, she faced her reflection, and stopped in amazement. The blue velvet corset accentuated her curves, sweeping over her breasts and making her waist appear tiny in comparison. Her breasts were encased in the velvet perfectly, two ripe globes whose roundness was accentuated by the extremely low-cut, scooping bodice. In fact, she could even see the tips of her nipples visible at the top. The lace modesty panel, as she'd originally thought, really wasn't for modesty, but instead featured an incredible view of the curving globes of her breasts and the valley in between. Looking lower, Evie realized the panties were high cut and now completely transparent, with only one arm of the snowflake covering her mound. The musky smell of her arousal filled the room. "So," she said shakily, "Do you like what you see?"

Rose was stunned. The bodice fit Evie like it had been painted on her. Rose realized that Evie's firm, round buttocks were only inches away from Rose's face, and she could feel the heat rising from her skin. Looking back into the mirror, Rose saw that the front of the panties were soaked with Evie's juices; she could see the outline of her mound and the beginning of her pussy lips. So Evie did want Rose as badly as she wanted her! The fact made her intensely happy, but she tried to keep her voice steady as she said, "You know what we Renn Faire girls use the valley in our cleavage for?"

"What?" Evie replied, meeting Rose's eyes again in the mirror.

"This." Rose stood up, taking the small dagger she always kept in her cleavage out and unsheathing it. In one quick, professional move, she slit down the lacings holding Evie's corset together. "Don't you think it's convenient?"

Evie couldn't reply as she felt the corset fall away. She felt Rose's trembling hands cup her naked breasts, and her touch, tentative, caressing, felt so good she couldn't say anything at all, couldn't even think. Evie leaned into Rose's body, feeling the contact of her velvet dress against her aroused nipples. Rose leaned in too, holding Evie up, then placing pressure on her shoulders to make her sit down. Evie and Rose both sat on the padded bench, Rose now lightly caressing Evie's beautiful face.

"Rose...you know I never have..." Evie tried to say, but was caught up by the intense look in Rose's eyes.

"Shh...don't talk. It's all ok." Holding Evie by the chin, Rose leaned towards her, looking deeply into her eyes. "Kiss me."

Evie felt Rose's warm lips meet her own, and an electric current thrilled in her veins. Her first lesbian kiss was everything she'd ever dreamed of in a kiss. It was everything she'd ever wanted, but never gotten, from a man; it was a complete arousal that burned her body and made her rub against the bench, blindly seeking the orgasm she knew was on its way. Their lips touched gently, each tasting the other, then sliding back and forth, tongues sipping at each other's mouths. It became more and more passionate, with Evie gasping for air as Rose slid her tongue into her mouth boldly, twining with Evie's own tongue. Rose tasted so incredibly good, so sweet....Evie was drowning in passion. Her juices soaked the bench beneath her pussy. Rose twined her fingers in Evie's hair, holding the back of her head, drawing her closer to her, and they felt their passion rise. Evie moaned.

I think you need me very badly," Rose whispered, huskily. Continuing to kiss Evie, she cupped one of Evie's breasts in her hand, teasing her nipple. "I think I am going to suck on your breasts and lick your pussy until you cum."

"Yes, please, yes, do it," Evie urged. She lay back against the bench and ground her soaking wet, panty clad pussy against Rose's knee, covered in velvet.

Rose laughed and looked into Evie's passion-filled clear blue eyes. Leaning over Evie where she lay on the bench, Rose felt the extreme pleasure that only making love can give come over her in waves. This was no ordinary woman. This was no ordinary event. She stowed away the thought until later, and kissed Evie harder, caressing her hard nipples until Evie arched her back and cried out, rubbing her pussy against Rose's knee again. "Bad girl," Rose said, and reached down and slapped Evie's pussy playfully. Rose kissed her way across to Evie's shell-like ear, tugging gently with her teeth on Evie's pierced hoop earring. She could feel the tremors shake Evie's body. She gently nibbled the outer lobe of Evie's ear, swirling her tongue into her ear to surprise Evie. Evie moaned, but not as much as she did when Rose gently licked and nibbled down Evie's neck, reaching a spot where she made one gentle, lingering bite.

"Oh my God! Rose!" Evie exclaimed, arching her back all the way off the bench and experiencing the most intense, mind-shattering orgasm she'd ever had. Then she realized she'd just been given an orgasm by a bite on the neck, and she shivered. What else did Rose have in store for her?

Rose felt Evie's orgasm and smiled. She couldn't stop licking and tasting her neck, that combination of fresh, clean scent combined with the smell of Evie's skin and her arousal. She could feel Evie's wetness soaking the fabric of her dress. It must have been a good orgasm, but she wanted to give her more. Delicately, she kissed down the side of her neck, stopping to nip at her collarbones and the tops of her shoulders, leaving a lingering kiss to the sides of the base of her throat. Rose could feel Evie's arousal beginning again. She gently caressed the Evie's sides with her fingertips, especially around the sides of her breasts. Once again, Evie's nipples tightened in arousal, and Rose smiled, lowering her mouth to Evie's breasts. With her fingers lightly caressing Evie's heated skin, she lightly kissed around Evie's nipples, licking upwards towards them, giving her small bites and nibbles. Evie gasped as Rose blew on the nipples, making them painfully hard and cold. Rose's hands then cupped Evie's breasts harder, bringing them up to her waiting lips. She licked one of Evie's nipples, then took it into her mouth, sucking hard. Evie tasted incredible. Rose marveled at how incredible Evie was, how passionate and responsive she was. She felt Evie's arms around her, holding her head down to her breast. She sucked and licked and nibbled both breasts, playing with them, holding them roughly together, pinching the nipples until they were harder than ever. Rose even ran her nails down both nipples as she kissed her way down Evie's stomach, marveling at the red lines she left in Evie's smooth white skin. Evie moaned, disappointed, as she realized that Rose's knee had left her pussy. "Don't worry, darling, you're fixing to get something even better," Rose whispered, biting lightly around Evie's belly button, tonguing it. Evie felt Rose's rough, hot tongue sliding in and out of her belly button and moaned.

"But...I want to..." Evie felt like she must feel Rose's body against hers, that she must please her in every way possible. Rose had given her intense pleasure, and now Evie wanted to give her the same pleasure.

"No. This is special. Besides, you can owe me one and pay me back later," Rose said, digging her nails ever so lightly into Evie's sides and running them down her hips. She breathed in the pure, aroused aroma of Evie, and all she could think of was tasting her, licking her. Without removing the sopping wet panties, Rose touched Evie lightly with one fingertip, teasingly running her down Evie's hot, pouting pussy lips, and back up again. Evie spread her legs wide for Rose, her pussy lips so aroused that they were almost around the thin strip of panty material. Rose dipped her finger in Evie's slick wetness, feeling her shudder, and holding her hips firmly down with her other hand. She pressed harder against the flimsy material, running her nuckles against Evie's pussy, up and down several times. Rose still never touched Evie's clit directly, instead alternating between the firm pressure of her knuckles and the teasing feel of her nails against the panty material covering her clit.

Evie began to shudder uncontrollably and push at the material of her panties, trying to take them off. "Please...please," she moaned, bucking her hips.

Rose could stand no more. She tore off her skirt, revealing her own black lace panties, also obviously wet in the center. She jerked at the knot on her bodice, cutting the laces with her knife. Peeling the rest of the corset off her, she revealed her freckled, exquisite, pear shaped breasts with large, aroused rosy nipples to Evie. "What do you think?" she asked hoarsely, hoping Evie would like what she saw.

"You're beautiful. And I want you so badly." Evie reached out her arms for Rose, wanting more than anything to feel Rose's skin against her own, feel her nipples rubbing against hers, to tumble on the floor with her, grinding pussy against pussy...

Rose parted Evie's knees roughly, then lightly bit the soft rise of her mound. "I want to taste you," she whispered. Her tongue dipped down between Evie's pussy lips, licking the material of her panties.

As Rose's tongue moved upwards, Evie finally felt it against the flesh of her aching pussy. "Oh Rose! That feels so good!" she screamed, nearly driving Rose insane with passion.

Rose tore the panties off Evie; thinking back on it later, she didn't even remember how it happened. All she remembered was driving her tongue deep into Evie's pussy, tasting her musky honey again and again, running the flat of her tongue against the pearl of Evie's aroused clit. She licked Evie hard, holding her down by wrapping both her arms around Evie's bucking hips. She buried her face in Evie's heavenly pussy, her face becoming covered with Evie's juices. Finally Rose simultaneously sucked Evie's clit, and thrust one finger up into Evie's vagina, rocking again and again to the same rhythm, then using two fingers and finding the nub of Evie's G spot, she dove Evie to a shuddering orgasm, lasting over several minutes. Rose could feel Evie's tight inner muscle spasms around her fingers, and the wetness that flowed afterwards was proof of how much Evie enjoyed it.

Evie had screamed herself hoarse, and didn't think she could strongly react to anything else, when she felt Rose suck hard on her clit and finger her at the same time. She could feel the hard inner contractions start, and saw stars, feeling her whole body shudder, her back arching, and, dimly, she could hear herself crying out. She felt something break inside herself, and the hardest spasm she'd ever had. What was that?

Rose collapsed on top of Evie, feeling her breasts push against Evie's breasts as she kissed her slowly. Had Evie enjoyed her first experience? Was it truly as good as it had seemed to Rose?

Evie sighed with contentment against Rose's lips. "Dearest, that was incredible," she whispered. Smiling lazily at Rose, Evie curled a section of Rose's hair around her finger. "You are magical. I just hope you don't "custom fit" your corsets for all your customers."

Rose smiled, a question in her hazel eyes. "What, you don't think all Miladies would enjoy this?"

"Well, I'm a bit possessive...I want to be youronly lady," Evie replied. Somehow, this moment, it just felt right. Even though they'd only known each other a few hours, she knew she wanted to make love to Rose for the rest of her life.

Rose arched an eyebrow, even though her heart was thumping like a schoolgirl with her first crush. "But how am I to make a living? My custom demands good service!" She pouted.

"And you'll give it to them," Evie promised, "but with embroidery alone." She reached behind Rose, pulling the cushion from the bench and tumbling them both to the carpeted floor. Evie landed first and she could feel Rose's body landing on top of hers, their breasts flat against each other, nipples rubbing. In the mirror, she could see both their bodies intertwined, and it aroused her. "Now let's see about that payback you were talking about..."

Punishment for the Crime

The thing in the tank beneath him was getting restless. He could hear it moving in the ooze that kept it alive, soft little keening cries only just audible through the thick, bullet proof glass. It was hungry and he, Kite, was its meal.

He squirmed slightly against the padded metal sling that held him suspended above the tank. It might have been comfortable if he wasn't facing the tank. The only things keeping him to the sling were the series of thick leather cuffs and his weight pressed against them painfully. His entire body ached with the stress of trying to keep his body tense.

Kite was completely naked, except for a blindfold, and the room he was in was being kept cold, presumably because the thing in the tank preferred it that way. Or maybe they just liked to see him shiver.

He could hear them too. The viewing public, waiting none too patiently for the moment his case was decided. Theft was a pathetic and petty crime and the Alderi people liked to punish its criminals accordingly. A page had been set up for him on the Criminal Punishment site and, eventually, enough votes would tally up on one side of the argument or the other and he would be acquitted or the thing in the tank got its meal. Kite had watched similar punishments being dealt out and he was ashamed to say he'd very much enjoyed the spectacle. Some people enjoyed it so much, they'd pay to watch from the gallery that surrounded the room Kite was hung in.

Kite could imagine the slick tentacles sliding up from the tank, leaving a trail of ooze up his inner thigh... He felt himself twitch in response to the thought and told himself to think about something else.

The problem was, he almost wanted the vote to go against him. He'd watched others be given to the creatures like the one below him and he'd watched the horror turn to reluctant then overwhelming pleasure. He'd watched them writhe, buck, scream for more. The only true punishment was the humiliation, in Kite's mind anyway. Kite had no-one to be humiliated by, no-one who'd judge him for craving those slick, sliding tentacles.

The thing sloshed around in its ooze and Kite wondered if it could sense his excitement. It did, after all, feed on cum, so perhaps it was sensitive to others emotions. Maybe it just detected his heart rate rising.

He hung there for another half an hour, listening to the shifting of butts on seats, small coughs and muted conversation. He guessed that many of the viewers in the gallery would be keeping themselves amused with vibrating butt plugs and dildos. Their calm, serene smiles would hide the fact they were building themselves slowly to the first of, they would hope, many wonderful orgasms. He had seen punishment sessions where the entire viewing gallery was one massive gangbang once the punishment really got going. Those sweet, innocent smiles were replaced with wicked grins, wide, open expressions of pure ecstasy and, of course, hidden completely behind someone's thrusting ass as they took a mouthful of cock.

Something hit the top of the glass tank with a dull thunk. The thing could definitely sense him struggling to keep calm. His cock was starting to get hard and he realised it must be showing because whispers came from the viewing gallery.

Suddenly, a cool female voice spoke. 'The vote has now closed. Kite Liro, you are sentenced to three hours with the Xylax, after which you will be free to go. Your punishment will begin in five minutes.'

A cheer went up from the viewing gallery and Kite felt his cock harden. He was going to get it. The best fuck of his life, here and now.

There was a click of machinery and then the sling was rotating, turning him round so he was sitting on it, like he was lying on a couch, his ass significantly lower than the rest of him. His legs were spread out and there was a large portion of the seat bit around his ass that was completely missing. The sling shifted further, keeping his ass low but bending his back slightly and tilting his head back. It was, Kite reflected, actually quite comfortable, like lying on the edge of his bed, with his head and shoulders dangling over the side.

The blindfold, a screen resting over his eyes, folded back and disappeared behind Kite's head.

Finally, the sling was moved upwards, until Kite was ten foot from the ground. He knew they did this purely to ramp up the tension before the moment of first contact.

The cool female voice came back after what felt like a minute to announce, 'Punishment will now commence.'

Kite heard, but couldn't see, the sound of the tank lid sliding back and then the ooze as it lapped against the sides. The gallery let out an 'ooo' and he watched a man above him, to his right bend, his partner over the viewing rail and slip several fingers into his ass. A woman further along also had her partner over the rail and was merrily adding weights to the man's nipple clamps. Kite could see his cock straining against a chastity cage. Kite looked left and saw two slaves sharing a double ended dildo as they looked down on him, their master watching over them with a small smirk.

He would have watched for longer but a cold, slimy touch on his ass diverted his attention. It slipped further up his leg, exploring him, leaving a trail of ooze as it went. The sensation might have been disgusting if Kite's mind hadn't been so firmly fixed on what it was going to feel like when that tentacle slipped inside of him. It was now at the top of his thigh then buried in his crotch, all too swiftly passing over his cock, although Kite thought it might have linger for a moment on the very tip which was probably slick with precum - he couldn't tell with his head tipped back. His cock felt cold, though, covered in ooze and he began to lose some of the hardness.

Another tentacle joined the first and went straight for his head. Kite saw it coming, the appendage a mottled black colour, completely smooth and tapered to a point. It slid over his short hair and down his forehead, using only the tip as if it knew this was a delicate area. It found his mouth but merely passed over his lips, oozing all the way and Kite found the ooze to be ever so slightly sweet and... sort of refreshing. It wasn't cloying or thick at all. He poked his tongue out from between his lips to get a proper taste. Definitely refreshing. Like a cool glass of water on a hot summer day.

The tentacle passed over his lips twice more before it delicately probed his lips, barely putting any pressure behind the action at all. Kite's lips parted for it and the tentacle probed further then backed off, allowing his lips to close. Then it was pressing against them again and again Kite let it open him. He could feel the other appendage slipping along his legs, testing, exploring.

The tentacle withdrew once more and returned and slowly, the thing fucked his mouth, pushing a little more inside of him every time, until he was taking five inches of tentacle and starting to gag on it. The moments were so slow that he had a good five seconds of no air before the tentacle slipped away. It was excruciatingly pleasurable. The slick, thick tentacle with its ooze, the inevitability of it, his body completely pinned, his mouth at the mercy of the creature. And so, so slow.

Then Kite began to notice the tip starting to bulge and he knew what happened next. Each tentacle had the ability to grow or shrink as it wished and each was very sensitive, especially when the thing in the tank expanded the area its nerve ends were touching.

The tentacle slowly grew a bulbous head as it fucked his mouth, until it could barely fit the girth through Kite's stretched lips. Perhaps sensing this, the tip stopped growing. It continued to slowly, gently but insistently slide the bulbous head in and out of Kite's mouth.

Meanwhile, the other tentacle had been joined by several others and they were slipping over his skin with increasing excitement, pulling at his fingers and winding round his ankles. One finally slipped in between his ass cheeks and Kite moaned into the tentacle but it refused to simply fuck him. Instead, the tentacle rubbed at the little nub of pink, sending shivers down Kite's spine and making his cock stand to attention.

Rub, rub, rub...

Kite opened his eyes and watched the man who'd been fingering his partner happily slide his cock in with a blissful expression that was probably accompanied by a sigh of happiness. The mistress with the weights was gleefully fucking her slave's mouth with a huge dildo, his mouth, like Kite's barely big enough. Kite looked left to the pair of slaves and was rewarded with the sight of each of them sliding down onto large alien looking dildos, their arms chained behind them, eyes alight with the sight of Kite and the creature. Their master was clearly bulging inside his trousers but seemed in no haste to do anything about it.

Kite watched him as the tentacle rubbed at his ass with a long length of itself, enough that his ass cheeks parted quite considerably. Then, without any warning, it slipped the very tip inside of him, just once. He moaned and the tentacle in his mouth twitched but the other went back to rubbing has ass as if he hadn't reacted. Then, less than ten seconds later, it did it again, pushing a little more inside. Kite moaned in protest as it removed the tip and this time, it responded, pushing itself back inside almost instantly, the ooze making the movement easy. And back again, pushing enough to widen his ass a good half inch.

Kite felt himself getting hard, almost painfully hard. He'd barely been touched and he was already ready. But he knew he wouldn't cum. The ooze was very clever. He hadn't known how it would taste but it was common knowledge that it was an inhibitor. He wouldn't be able to cum until the thing released the counter chemical. He'd be kept on the brink until it was completely and utterly ready to harvest its meal from him and he'd seen punishments where the thing hadn't let the criminal cum for over an hour.

And he had three hours with this one.

The tentacle probed further and further each time and now it was starting to test him. He'd trained his ass to be able to take some big cocks but, of course, the tentacle could go as big as it wanted. He was going to be stretched to his limit. The excitement boiled up inside him until he didn't know what was longing and what was due to the tentacle probing him.

Just as the one in his mouth had, the tip of the tentacle started to grow and the feeling of it moving inside of him made his balls clench and his cock twitch. It kept growing and growing, until it felt like a cannonball moving slowly up and down inside of him. Then the ball lengthened as more of the tentacle expanded and Kite felt ridges on the length, rippling against the walls of his ass, catching at him pleasurably.

It didn't withdraw itself any longer but moved inside up and down, up and down inside of him, getting ever wider, the ridges becoming more pronounced until Kite wanted to bite the mass of tentacle in his mouth. It was too much, too amazingly good. His ass felt like one big aching nerve, his cock just pulses of pure, glorious agony. All he needed was the silky, mocking voice of a master to tell him he deserved none of the pleasure, that he must wait for the gift his master was going to so generously give him, that he was such a fucking slut to enjoy being debased like this, on display for all to see. The master's voice would get quieter, his lips so close to Kite's ear as he whispered the truth. 'You wanted to get caught, didn't you? You didn't even really want that bottle of rum. You wanted this. To be watched as you're used for the piece of ass you are.'

Kite spasmed in the sling, unable to get away from the relentless, slow fucking. He'd never seen a creature go this slowly before. It was as if it wasn't particularly hungry and was instead, happy to take its merry time. Kite was desperate for release or more or both. Anything to relieve the tension in him.

The thing gave him more. The lump of tentacle in his ass started moving faster just as the one in his mouth shrunk a little in size and began fucking his mouth as fast as it could. It was less than a minute before the tentacle in his ass was going just as quickly and Kite realised his mistake in wishing for more. He needed - needed - to cum. His body arched against the leather bonds, straining for release, his cock and balls a mass of desperation. The ridges thrummed against the inside of his ass, the slippery tentacle in his mouth stretching his lips wide and filling him with ooze. He could feel more ooze dripping from his ass as the tentacle thrust in and out. It dripped into the tank below with little 'plink' sounds.

Master, please! Kite thought desperately, clinging to what little remained of himself. He was pure sensation and need and aching, aching pleasure.

This will not be the last time you say that today, said a voice into his mind as a liquid filled his mouth and dribbled down his cheeks.

Kite came with such force it was almost painful. He hadn't noticed the tentacle that waited but now, as it clamped onto his cock, settling happily around his head, the sensations as he pulsed against its tight embrace were overwhelming. His body spasmed and shivered and bucked until he collapsed back against the sling, unable to lift a finger. The tentacles shrank back to their original sizes and withdrew.

Mmmm, very good, said the voice in his mind.

Master? Kite thought weakly, his brain swarming with soft heat.

Oh, very much so, said the voice. I think I might request you as a permanent meal source, it purred, one tentacle wrapping lazily around his foot.

Why? Kite thought.

I like the way you think. Not many wish for a master while they're with me.

I will serve you any way you wish me to, Kite thought honestly, still shivering.

Call me by my name and I will make you forever mine. Call me as you did at the end.

Master, Kite thought without hesitation, and was rewarded with a tentacle slipping around his neck and tightening possessively.

Apology

I'm really sorry I haven't been able to update.. I've been really sick but I'm getting better

Well that's about it...

And yes you can make requests of what you want to see

DORM ROOM DICK DOWN 1

As Requested....

When I was a freshman in college, there was a guy on my floor who made me very uncomfortable. His name was Simon and he was tall, burly, and looked 30. It turns out he'd actually repeated a grade for sports and was a year older, but it seemed more like 10.

The reason he made me nervous was two-fold. For starters, he had a habit of looking at me funny whenever we were together. Whether it be a floor activity, drinking with the boys, or simply hanging out, I'd always catch him eyeing me, making me blush with hot nerves. Which brings us to the second reason I was afraid of him: raw attraction.

I knew I was gay but it was the 80s and the closet was safe. That still couldn't stop me from shivering with secret desire when I saw him on the first day. He was exactly my type: big, strong, always in his cowboy boots and hat like he was still in west Texas.... Damn, Simon was fine. But his big muscles only fueled my fear of getting caught drooling since he was a tough dude who could snap me like a twig! I tried to play it chill as we settled in but remained wary around him.

Our floor had a communal shower and one day me and the boys were having a rinse. Simon was there too, to my dismay, so I had to avoid spying his football-player body, lest I pop a boner in front of everyone.

While facing the nozzle and washing my hair, Simon called out, "yo, Matty, why'd you never tell us you have such a big ass!"

The boys all cracked up while I blushed profusely. Simon and I didn't interact much on account of my fear and this was one of the first things he'd said to me. How humiliating for it to be a comment about my butt! And on top of it all, he wasn't lying. I do have a big butt and it's always been a source of shame. I'd been made fun of for it before but thought those days were over.

"I'm serious, Matty," he continued, again calling me by a childhood nickname I was trying to drop. "It's like a girl's butt, all big and round. And barely a hair on there! Mine looks like a damn forest!"

He turned around to shake his thick, hirsute ass and everyone howled. I burned with humiliation but took it in stride, hoping to not look like a crybaby. My reaction seemed to work as everyone got over it; well, everyone but Simon. When we exited he wrapped his arm around my shoulder, an act that was quite intimate since we were both naked.

"I'm not kidding, man, that ass is something to be proud of. Matches that girly little dick of yours, too," he added with a sly wink. I dropped my head in shame because he was again astute.

"Awww, cheer up, buttercup, I'm just payin' you a compliment," he said while holding my chin in a joking manner. "Well, see you around, girly butt!"

SMACK

Before Simon walked away he spanked my ass harder than it ever had been, making it ripple like jello. The thunderous clap echoed through the bathroom and the stinging sensation remained for nearly two minutes. When I got to my room, I ran to the mirror

and dropped my towel. Upon turning around I saw an enormous hand print painted across my entire milky buttcheek!

"Oh my god..." I shuddered while viewing it at different angles.

As I inspected Simon's print, my dick began to rise... I couldn't believe he'd marked me like that, branded his big hand on my naked flesh! It felt like it wasn't even my skin anymore, like it was his, and his bizarre comments in the shower only made me hornier. Even though I knew he was just teasing me like he did with everyone, the spank made it so much more lewd. I jerked off in front of the mirror while tracing over the red, welted lines, then spewed on the floor.

The following days were normal, but I couldn't stop thinking about my encounter with Simon; his big hands marking me... We still hung out in a group and they'd all forgotten about my fat ass--except Simon, of course.

Those pants are a little tight, don't ya think, girly butt?" he asked while sneaking up from behind one evening.

He planted his meaty paws right on my cheeks and I jumped.

"Shut up, man!" I whined with a weak punch, tacitly accepting my new nickname.

"Whatever you say, girly butt!"

Simon didn't stop his teasing and actually ramped it up, finding ways to grope me whenever we were together. His constant touching was weird but it all felt like a running joke so I just let it happen. If he exited with a spank, which often occurred, I'd sprint to my room to check it in the mirror. Even through my jeans he would leave a faint handprint. I cherished them....

"Come on, man, quit it..." I begged at a party the next weekend.

"Just another second, Matty, not much longer."

Simon and I were in the kitchen grabbing drinks when his roughhousing got more aggressive than usual. He pushed me up against the sink and his hands went straight to my buns, where he started squeezing and kneading.

"So big...." he muttered.

"Come on, dude, cut it out!" I pleaded.

We were both drunk and I didn't know if this was just another one of his games.

"Don't get all bitchy with me, girly butt. I'm just giving you the attention you deserve."

"Duuuude, that's enough. Pleeease...."

My dick swelled as Simon drunkenly humped and groped me. I got nervous someone would see and was also afraid of my own homosexuality, so I tried squirming away but he cut me off.

"Don't ever pull away from me!" he ordered sternly in a tone I'd never heard. It scared me.

Okay... sorry..." I whimpered in defeat, aware he could easily overpower me.

"Good boy."

I stood pathetically and allowed Simon to fondle my butt for another minute before he grabbed us two beers. He then wrapped his arm around me and walked us back out to the party like nothing had happened.

My memories of his actions were hazy but I knew something weird had occurred. I wasn't yet too afraid to be around him, but was now on guard whenever he was nearby. In the showers though, nothing could protect my naked butt from his greedy paws.

"Didn't think I'd see you in here," Simon smirked as he sauntered into the bathroom.

I'd been enjoying my privacy but now was completely on edge.

"Calm down, I'm not gonna hurt you," he said genuinely, clearly noticing my nerves.

I appreciated his kindness and went back to washing myself. Forgetting who was across from me, I turned to rinse my hair. Big mistake.

Ooooowee!!" Simon whistled when my rump was in full view. "Now that's a peach right there!"

I blushed and quickly turned back so he couldn't see.

"Oh come on now, baby, don't be shy. Let me see that big ass of yours. There's no harm."

"Dude, cut it out...." I muttered, if only to put up my usual front.

"Come onnnn, just a peek," he winked cheekily. It was sort of cute how badly he wanted to see it.

I was relishing in his compliments and they must've gone to my head. Craving more, I slowly turned for Simon. Once my rear was displayed he hooted and hollered like a soldier at a USO show.

"What a fuckin' rump!" he smiled. "Now you're not gonna let Ol' Simon leave barehanded, are ya sweetheart?"

He gazed at me like a boy with a crush and my body turned scarlet. I looked over my shoulder at him with trepidation, my back still arched, but gave no response. I guess silence was better than "no" so Simon waltzed over to my shower head.

"Hey, girly butt," he soothed as his hairy chest lined up with my back.

His paws of course went directly to my bare cheeks, his first encounter with my naked flesh since the initial spank. He began to gently manipulate my jiggly buns and it was intoxicating. I had to try not to melt back.

"Have you had enough...?" I asked nervously after a minute. Even though I loved his touch, the experience was petrifying.

"I'll let you know when I'm done, sweet cheeks. I'm gonna touch this ass as long as I want to and you're gonna stand here and let me. Don't act like you don't like this."

He must've seen my dick, which was now rock solid and pointing up. His was evidently in a similar state and I could feel it grazing my spine.

"Mmmmm..." I moaned softly as he squeezed and smooshed my cheeks.

His finger got curious though, as all men's do, and was soon tapping against my tight pucker.

TAP TAP TAP

I could hear him splashing against my wet hole.

"Mmmm... s-stop..." I whispered, trying desperately to pretend I didn't love it. Each touch was electric.

"Shhhhh...." he hushed while pushing his nail in.

I gasped and started squirming but he just held my chest and kept burrow-ing. I was panting at the first knuckle, groaning through the second. By the third I was positively bucking as his long finger curled perfectly against my sensitive prostate, filling up my pink tunnel.

"Uhhh.... Mmmmm!!" I moaned as he dug deeper.

"I bet I'm touchin' spots your little girly fingers can't reach, huh?"

How did he know?!! I didn't respond but we both knew it was true. I fingered myself often but had never come close to the heights of pleasure he was taking me. Each prostate scrape another crashing wave.

"Gonna be hittin' all your spots once I get my thick rod up there, Matty boy. You're gonna love it."

He said it with such confidence, such absolute surety that he would even-tually fuck me. It made me feel weak and owned, like I had no say in my own fate.

"C-come on, dude...." I stuttered through jittering teeth. "That's enough."

The excavation became too intense and my internalized homophobia couldn't handle it anymore. Though I still didn't push him off, Simon finally pulled his finger out and held my butt.

"Such a sweet, tight ass," he contended. "I want it smooth though next time, alright girly butt? No hair between those little cheeks."

He slid his digits up my crack and pinched the few blonde hairs that grew there. I had no idea how to respond but Simon left the bathroom whistling before I could think of anything.

My mind was now a mess. I stood in the shower with a painfully erect cock, fully aware it was in this condition because a man just sodomized me. The guilt and shame of enjoying his pleasure ate away at me, but it didn't stop me from jerking off the second he left. I tried to think of anything but Simon, but my thoughts raced back to his hands, his fingers, his sheer dominance. He was so hard to resist.....

As more days passed, I made an effort to avoid him. This wasn't easy since the dorm was small, but if I knew he was gonna be somewhere I made other plans. My behavior became erratic and I couldn't think straight, constantly pining for a man I feared. If I did see Simon, he'd smile at me like nothing happened and I'd scurry away like a frightened mouse. But I should've known I couldn't hide forever. I should've known when a man wants something, he gets it.

After studying late one night, I walked back to the dorm and arrived at my room. While unlocking, a hairy hand planted itself above my head. I turned around quickly and held my key like a weapon.

"Calm down, sweet cheeks, don't get your panties in a twist. It's just me."

"Oh, Simon.... Hey..."

"You know you can't avoid me forever, right?"

"I wasn't avoiding you..." I lied, but he wasn't listening and instead pulled us into my room, then shut the door and locked it.

"Ummm... Simon, I-"

"Shhhhhh, don't get upset. It's okay if you liked it."

"Nooo, but I-"

"Shhhhhh...."

Simon shushed me with a bear hug, paws instantly groping their favorite derrière. Over the pants wasn't enough though so he began unbuckling my belt.

"Dude, wait, come on..." I whimpered, but it didn't stop him.

Once the belt was gone he easily slipped off my jeans. Of course my tighty whities couldn't stay, so he stripped those too, followed by a quick lift of my shirt.

"Aaahhh, much better," he sighed when his hands returned. "Oh, what's this?"

He'd inevitably traveled inward to find the source of my sexual heat and smiled when he felt around. To my utter embarrassment, I'd followed his instructions and shaved my ass crack. I did it alone in my room so no one could see then spent the night tracing my fingers around my porcelain snatch. How did he know I would love being smooth?!?

Simon tilted my chin up, concupiscence glowing in his eyes. "Did you shave for me, sweetheart?"

I could only look down in response but we both knew I did. Shivering in his arms, I felt so vulnerable and submissive. This guy who'd been molesting me for weeks was now in my room, fully clothed while I stood naked getting groped. The situation was so ego-shattering that I could only surrender; I melted into Simon's hug and laid my cheek meekly on his white polo. My surrender was met with a lurch from his khaki's which admittedly made me happy.

"W-what are you doing...?" I asked when he let go and started walking behind me.

Although I secretly loved his butt touches I was still wary of going too far. I simply wasn't ready for that.

"I just wanna do something, sweetie, don't worry..."

"Ummm... okay... Uhhh.. Simon...? S-Simon... Oooohhhh... Uh! UHH! S-Simon! Simon!! W-what are you doing? Ohhh, MMM! SIMON!!"

"Quiet down, babe, unless you want everyone to hear."

I tried to muffle my wanton cries as my friend did something I'd never even imagined! I saw him crouch behind me and spread my cheeks. "Such a sweet hole," he said. Then he blew on it a few times which sort of tickled and sent me on my toes. But when he leaned forward and his wet tongue touched my quivering hole, his coarse beard scraped my soft skin, I nearly lost it.

"UUHNNNGGG SIMON!" I squealed as he gave me a tongue lashing to remember.

Through ingenious manipulation he coaxed me forward until I was lying prone on the carpet. From here he had an all-access pass to my smooth taint, balls and hole. He licked up the whole zone, scratching his beard across it as he traveled, sending jolts of pure pleasure inside me. He deftly spread my legs while working, and as my hips opened I found my back arching, my ass grinding to meet him.

"What a delicious butt," he whispered to himself while slipping a wet finger inside.

"OH!!"

It was exactly what I'd needed. Since he'd started rimming, my butt felt a unique emptiness, a wanton desire to be filled. His finger was lovely and understood my needs, yet somehow I still craved more. When one digit became two I was briefly satisfied, but that deep, aching hunger still existed, and was growing!

"Look at your little hole chewin' on my fat fingers. So cute."

He spanked my bum to commend me for flexing my internal muscles. Each squeeze increased the pressure on my boy button and felt fantastic!

"Ummm... Simon..." I whispered cautiously when I heard his belt jingle a minute later. The sound shot me out of my reverie and I was back on guard.

"Shhh, baby, it's okay. I'm just gettin' more comfortable. You just lie down and let me take care of you."

I laid my cheek back on the carpet and looked at the wall while Simon slid his pants down. My butt was clenched when he returned, but with tactical pinches and kisses he again coaxed my thighs open. My eyes shut in blissful joy when his beard returned.

"You've just got the nicest ass," he complimented as his massive body moved up to cover mine. His mouth was now by my ear. "The nicest, tightest, girliest little ass...."

His neck kisses turned me to putty while I squirmed below. The passionate jerking caused my legs to spread so Simon took advantage. He locked his knees inside mine and continued to push until my legs were in a wide V. My hole was so exposed now and I could feel his enormous dick grinding up against it.

"Uhhh.. S-Simon..."

"Sshhhhh, baby, it's okay. I'm not gonna put it in. I just like feelin' you squirm under me."

It was comforting to know he wasn't gonna fuck me so I relaxed and let him play with my body. After a few minutes though he went too far and started poking my tiny hole with his pole.

"C-come on, dude, seriously..." I whimpered futilely.

"Don't worry, baby, you're okay. I just like pokin' it with my dick. You have to admit it feels good, huh?"

I guess he had a point... Every time his tip pushed against my wrinkles I experienced deep pangs of longing inside me--insatiable cravings. I relaxed again and allowed him to prod, though after a minute I noticed his tip was suspiciously slick.

"I just put a little lube on so I can slide around on your hole. It's nothing, don't worry," he ensured.

"Okay...." I muttered nervously with re-clenched cheeks. A few lubey gropes pried them right back open.

"Fuuuuck this feels good," Simon groaned once he'd gotten into a rhythm.

His cock was sufficiently slick and was now gliding between my buns like a hot dog. It also felt great for me since each time his head crossed my pucker he'd give it some love. He pushed against it gently and the pressure was exquisite, even if I was afraid to lose my cherry. I knew Simon wouldn't fuck me unless I let him, though.

"Ow! Don't put it in!" I complained when a playful poke went a bit too far.

His wet tip had almost punched through my barrier and I quickly clenched to expel him. This did little to deter Simon though. He immediately lined his head back up to my hole and held me tight.

"Relax, Matty, I'm not gonna put it in," he persuaded.

All it took was a couple beard nuzzles for my muscles to relax again. His bulbous tip was prodding against my hole now, ever so slightly breaking through the air tight sphincter. I kept trying to clench to push him out but Simon's manhandling made it hard to move.

"Just relax, Matty, just relax."

He kept knocking against my door but was met with firm resistance.

"Come on, Matty, you know it's gonna happen," he whispered hypnotically. "Just relax.... Let me in, Matty, come on. Let me in..."

His constant pushing was hard to fend off and the simultaneous kissing and licking made it impossible. Slowly, I felt my walls give in as I could no longer hold back his battering ram.

"UHHH!!!" I cried when my sphincter finally loosened. Simon's tip broke straight through.

"There we go," he soothed while stroking my hair. "That wasn't so hard, huh?"

"Come on, man, pleeeaaassseee!" I moaned.

His tip was fucking giant and really hard to accommodate. Fortunately he'd used a lot of lube and gotten me loose with the rimjob, so I was more in shock than pain. In fact, as my hole molded to his helmet, it actually felt pretty good....

"You like my tip in your sugar hole?"

When I didn't respond he pulled out and reinserted. This elicited a loud squeal which I hoped couldn't be heard by others. Gravity started to do its job and the head was followed by the first shaft inch of many.

"Hhhnnnngg!!! Duuude!!! Take it out, come on!" I pleaded. "It's too big!!!"

I wasn't actually in much pain but the whole situation had me rattled. I mean seriously, a dick was in my ass! I was getting buttfucked! Simon didn't hear any of my pleas and just kept working his way in.

"God... I knew I was gonna fuck this ass," he gloated. "The second I saw this thing in the showers I said to myself, 'I'm gonna fuck that ass.' And look at me now!"

I was both humiliated and flattered to know I'd been a conquest. I also felt terribly submissive to Simon, understanding that the reason I was here getting fucked was because he wanted it. Once he had his eyes on me, it was only a matter of time until it happened. There was nothing I could've done to stop him.

"Unnggghhh!" I moaned more passionately than before as my fate was becoming sealed.

"Listen to those cute little sounds. So girly and sweet. Gimme another, baby."

Simon pulled his dick out and eased it back in slowly, drawing out a needy cry as his descent reached my throbbing prostate.

"There we go, that's what I like to hear. Those soft little whimpers."

DORM ROOM DICK DOWN 2

He pulled out and pushed in again, this time sending in a full five inches. My stretched walls sang with joy! The sensation of being filled, the intense pleasure of my nerve bundle being jammed, all while laying under this hairy beast was amazing!

"Uh! Uh! Uh!" I squeaked with each inch.

After another minute of humping and squirming, I finally felt them: his nuts. They were mashed up against my taint which meant he was balls deep, and boy did I feel it!

"OoooooOoOoO!! Uhhhh!! Simon! Take it out, dude! Take it out!! It's so fucking big!!" My ass spasmed as I tried to expel the foreign object.

"Fuuuck, that feels so good. Keep squeezin' your hole for me, baby. Milk my dick."

Shit! My struggles only turned him on!

"Unnhhh!!! Unnnnnnhhhh!!!!"

I was in fight or flight mode, scrambling like a maniac, but Simon held me still in his bear grip.

"Shhhh, baby, quiet down. I got you, I got you..."

He kissed all along my neck, relaxing my body. It calmed me down and we laid quietly while my insides molded to him. When they finally did it actually felt really good--being all stuffed up. My prostate was stimulated beyond belief and with each squeeze along his shaft I received more pleasure.

But it still wasn't lost on me that I was utterly impaled, unable to move while Simon claimed me. I felt like a stuck pig, a kebob, and even though getting fucked is the most emasculating act, it felt wonderful.

There you go, sweetie, you're alright," he comforted while stroking my face. "I'm all up inside you now. All 8 inches, just like I knew I would."

He maneuvered his head so we were eye to eye and continued to speak sweetly while brushing my bangs to the side.

"You made it so easy for me, Matty. Let me come right in and take you over. Never even fought me. Not once." He kissed my forehead. "Is that cuz you know your place, baby?"

I cringed and tried to turn away but it was impossible. It was so painful to admit that I wanted this, that I wanted to be fucked in the ass like a bitch. But that ship had already sailed. I was a butt boy now, so I nodded pathetically at Simon.

"That's right, baby, you know your place. Under me with spread legs. Just where you're 'sposed to be."

Simon slowly withdrew his cock and the tight suction caused an embarrassingly loud plop. He chuckled and slid back in, then began a series of mouth-watering grinds. They were slow and controlled, each calm thrust dominating my psyche. Simon never let me look away while he took me.

"UUUHHHH!!!" I wailed with sheer ecstasy as his cock drove deeper, punching my prostate until it bruised.

He shoved two fingers in my mouth and told me to suck. I was glad he did because he then sped up, yanking his whole horsecock out with each hump before ramming it back in. He eventually had to cover my mouth which forced me to breathe through my nose. I was getting plowed, Simon's sweat dripping onto me, his face red with passion, mine frozen in terror and ecstasy.

"Get up," he huffed after a bit more fucking.

He'd pulled out and stood up. I looked back at him with wild, confused eyes as he fully removed the jeans that had been around his ankles.

"W-what?"

"Let's go, let's go. I wanna fuck you proper on the bed."

My legs were still splayed and my hole was gaped and sore. It must have looked so loose and sloppy--freshly-fucked. It was difficult to move but with a lift from Simon I got on my feet. I felt so weak and small, wobbling timidly with a fucked-open hole while he denuded for part 2.

He whipped his shirt off then guided me towards the bed. In our privacy, I stared greedily at his thick, strong, hairy body. His muscles weren't ripped but damn he looked manly. While crawling back towards the pillows, I was half trying to escape another plowing, half eagerly preparing myself.

"Keep those legs spread, sweetie. I don't want you closin' up on me."

Simon pressed my thighs out while shimmying his sturdy hips between them. Once he was comfy, he locked the backs of my knees into the crooks of his arms.

"Look how natural you are on your back with your legs spread," he cooed. "I'm gonna take you just like a man takes his girl now, Matty. Like a little virgin bride."

"Uhhh... Uh!! S-Simon! Please! Please.... go slow....."

I'd long admitted defeat and now just hoped my abused hole received gentle treatment.

"I'll go as slow as you like," he whispered huskily, then dipped down to kiss me while gliding in his tip.

"Oooo!!! Si-"

He cut my groans off with sultry sucks and bites. Spearing his tongue in repeatedly, he took ownership of my mouth while simultaneously claiming my butt--the butt he knew was his.

"You've got such a sweet ass," he groaned while grinding in deep. "You like when I'm all up inside you, Matty? You like my big dick up your girly butt?"

He shook his hips at full depth to tease me internally.

"Yeah...." I admitted bashfully. He smiled and gave me another kiss.

"I knew you'd like it. That girly butt of yours was made to be stuffed."

"Mmmm!!! Uhhh!!" I cried with pleasure.

I hated to accept it but he was right. I was born to get fucked. Laying under him with my legs spread felt so natural. So right.

"I'm gonna be fuckin' this girly ass whenever I want to from now on, okay Matty? You're my little girlfriend now."

I wanted to cry I was so humiliated, but the only sounds emitted were of pure desire.

"You got that?" he asked with a powerful hump.

"Y-yes....!"

"Yes what?" He slowed down and was now smirking at me.

He grasped my smaller, erect cock with a lubey hand and squeezed.

"OOooooOoooO, Simon!"

"Yes what?" he asked again, gliding up and down my length. He circled his slick palm around my sensitive tip and pulled lightly on my ballsack.

"Unnnnnhhhh!!" Between the insane prostate stimulation and jerking off, I was so close to busting. "Y-yes! I'm your girlfriend!!"

"Yes. You. Are." he panted between thrusts. "And don't you forget it!!"

Simon threw his whole body forward and flexed his muscular ass. At this depth the pleasure was divine and my explosion instantly milked into his fist.

"Aaaaahhhh!!! AHH! AHHH!!! SIIIIMMMMOONN!!!"

My orgasm was so much more powerful when forced out by a huge dick. With each squirt my walls shuddered and squeezed around his girth, intensifying my pleasure while surely giving him a gushy massage. He remained at the hilt, impaling me fully as I squirmed and writhed and came. My spasms must've set him off because soon Simon was bellowing, neck veins popped while he strained his head to the ceiling.

"FUUUUCKKKK!!!!!"

Sweat dripped onto my chest and mixed with my spilled seed. We both lay there panting, Simon's slick body now flush with my chest, my semen absorbing into his hairy stomach. My smile felt permanent, my heart rate near bursting, adrenaline surging while I took it all in. Simon finally lifted his head and brushed away my damph

air.

"Mmmmmm..... that was fuckin' perfect...." he said with an exhausted, goofy grin.

"Ha... Yeah..." I chuckled back in awe.

Simon slowly slid his wilting cock out and I could feel his seed drip from my pounded-out hole. I tried to squeeze to not make a mess but was simply too gaped.

"Guess you'll just have to wash the sheets tomorrow," he laughed while standing up to grab a towel.

He came over and wiped me down then laid back in bed. I was still too drained to move so he threw my limp body onto his chest and started petting my back.

"You'll have to stop by and grab my laundry before you wash the sheets. You know, since you're my girlfriend and all now."

"Mmmmm okay, Simon...." I whispered in a daze. I didn't even know what I was agreeing to while nuzzling into him. I was still on a cloud.

"You know you're mine now, right, Matty?" he asked while stroking my cheek.

"Mmhmm...." I replied sleepily with closed eyes.

"I was serious about earlier," he continued, kissing my head until I looked at him. "That holes mine now, okay, baby? Whenever I want it."

"I know....." I responded meekly, kissing his hand.

"You're gonna be such a good girlfriend," he sighed happily while flipping me to little spoon.

"Oohhh... Simon...! A-again....?"

"Whenever I want," he reminded, pulling my leg up for easier access.

I tried my best to relax while he slid his greasy dick around my blown-out pucker. He fingered and played with it, circling around my newly-formed lips, then even made me touch it. My hole was wet and puffy, dilated and leaking jizz. It felt like the wet cunts I'd fingered at parties. A sloppy, lubricated gash waiting to be filled.

"Oooo... Simon...." I contended when his dick got all the way in.

It took a lot less effort than before and once he was settled the pleasure was immediate. I felt like he was back home, so I squeezed to welcome him. Simon wrapped his hairy arms around my chest, trapping my slimmer ones inside. He then held me like a puppet while humping, first slowly then more quickly as his passion increased. I couldn't jerk myself off in this position and evidently Simon didn't care to, so I just had to lay there as a warm hole for my "boyfriend" while he got his second nut.

"FUCK!" he huffed when he finally reached the peak.

My hard pecker was bouncing wildly with each buck, begging for a feel so I could get off. But once Simon drained his balls he held my hands and stayed firmly parked. I squirmed to get his softening cock out but he just pulled me tighter.

"I wanna sleep inside you," he whispered while interlocking our fingers.

"Okay...." I replied submissively, understanding that I wouldn't get off again tonight.

I accepted that as Simon's girlfriend there were going to be times I'd just have to lay there and take it. But as long as he gave me orgasms like the one earlier, I knew it would be worth it.

"Night, girly butt," he whispered with a kiss to my skull.

"Night, Simon," I said with a squeeze from both my hand and sphincter.

In the morning, I awoke to a lubey hand pawing my crack. As I groggily turned to look back, Simon was already inserting himself.

"W-wait..." I asked, still terribly sore from the night before. My hole felt wrecked and abused.

"Don't got time to wait, sweetheart, I got class in an hour."

Simon pushed forward and I gasped into his well-placed hand. He fucked slowly to open me up, and even though my prostate was exhausted it still enjoyed the attention.

"Hop up here, ride me," Simon said while pulling me onto his hips.

He held me down as I straddled him, my hands now on his hard, hairy pecs. I tried to stay seated but he lifted me until my butt was hovering over his piercing sword. Simon slowly guided my hips down and his big tip hit my wet lips. I subconsciously squeezed and gave his dick sloppy kisses as he shimmied inside.

"OoOoooOoo..." I sighed when he pulled me all the way down.

My knees were on the bed, asscheeks planted on his warm skin. Simon smiled and started bouncing, meeting me with his hips as we got into a rhythm. My dick was rock hard now and Simon jerked it with his slick hand.

"Ahhhhh! Fuuuckkkk!" I cried as he stroked my sensitive shaft.

I'd only cum once so far and was desperate to get off. Simon started pounding and each thrust set off a shockwave, emanating from my g-spot all the way down to my toes. The pressure was too great and my prostate bursted, followed by my walls choking and constricting his massive serpent.

"Oh fuuuckk!!" We groaned in unison while ejaculating, me onto his chest, him into my sloppy hole.

After calming down Simon pulled me off and set me on the floor. He sat on the side of the bed, legs spread, his fat, wet cock dangling between. He grabbed my shoulder and pushed me to the carpet.

"You gotta clean me up now, baby," he instructed once I got on my knees.

I hadn't yet sucked a dick and thought it was gross for my first time to be straight out of my ass. But there was something strangely exciting about performing such a debased act, and it didn't look dirty.... so I leaned forward and kissed his dripping tip.

"That's it, get it all," he coached while I licked the slimy shaft.

He told me to open up then plopped his softening meat in. It was still larger than mine when flaccid and the way his spongy flesh filled up my whole mouth was incredible. I began sucking harder, bobbing my head to give Simon the pleasure he deserved.

"That's it," he contented as his tube steeled back to 8 inches.

I loved feeling him harden in my mouth, hearing his moans when I used good technique. Simon put his hands on my hair and slowly fed me his penis. My cock was rising again at the lewd activity so I went to jerk it, but he gently kicked my hands away and told me to focus on him.

"I'll make you cum later, Matty, don't worry. You like it more when you're filled up anyways, right?"

"Mmhmm," I nodded, still focused on giving head.

"Good boy. Now I want you to swallow this all when I shoot, alright? I'm makin' a little breakfast for you."

He fucked my face quickly before cumming, yanking my head till drool sputtered. The rough treatment turned me on so much I thought I might bust without even touching myself! But Simon had other plans and shoved my head down till my nose tickled his pubes.

"Aaaaahhhhhh....." he sighed happily while draining a third load inside me.

I coughed after he pulled out, cum sticking to every surface of my mouth and throat. He handed me some water and I rinsed, then I stayed on my knees while Simon got dressed.

"I gotta head out now, Matty, but I'll see you after class, okay? I'm gonna leave my extra key here so you can grab my laundry. Hang it all up after too, would you, babe?"

"Yes, Simon..." I agreed, still in a daze from the blowjob, the buttfucking, everything!

"Great! I'll catch ya later. And don't go jerkin' that little thing without me, alright? I'll be back to help you out."

"Okay...." I replied with a shy smile. To be honest, I couldn't wait to see him again.

After my morning classes, I returned to the dorms to wash our stuff. When I opened Simon's door, a musky, masculine scent flooded my nostrils. The smell permeated the room and only became stronger as I got closer to his hamper. Dipping my nose, the delectable scent of his earthy balls wafted in and nearly made me drool. Mmmmm.

Before leaving with his clothes, I decided to sniff a pair of underwear. I'm usually not one for smells but the earthy musk accumulated in the area that housed his package was intoxicating. I pressed them to my nostrils and swooned while inhaling his delicious man smell.

I felt sort of silly doing Simon's laundry, being his girlfriend, but figured it was worth it. My ass craved his dick, I needed another one of those crazy orgasms only he could give me. Fortunately, Simon was equally horny and raced back to the dorms after class. I was in his room putting away his folded clothes when I heard the key slide in. My hole twitched in anticipation for what would come next.

"Hey, girly butt. I love seein' a pretty thing like you waitin' for me after a long day."

Simon put his bag down and came over for a hug. I went straight to his arms and rested my head on his hard chest. I wasn't sure how we were gonna keep things secret from the rest of the dorm, but if I got even a few more moments like this it would all be worth it.

GIRL'S NIGHT OUT 1

"D amn, I'm running late."

Liyah looked at the time on her cell phone with a bit of disgust, then lifted her trucker cap and smoothed down her long, straight jet-black hair. Adjusting the hat and accompanying sunglasses to her comfort, she slipped her cell back in her purse and walked up the last step of the Astor Place train stop. She dressed casually, yet trendy as would befit both her looks and the neighborhood. Her baby t-shirt looked even smaller than it was with her long, lean torso, and the fact she had D-cup breasts would have made her shirt seem downright slutty on an extrovert. In actuality, Liyah was shy and reserved. She just didn't mind the extra bit of attention she received nowadays. Always considered somewhat of an "ugly duckling" during the teen years, she was enjoying her new found beauty.

In a concession to the warm weather, she wore a pair of short shorts on her narrow hips that showed off her long caramel legs as she walked over to the restaurant. She was careful not to wear them too short, lest people get to know her *too* well.

Glancing up through her shades, she noticed the place coming up ahead. It was a regular spot for her and her friend Nikki for their regular hangout sessions. Walking across the street to her destination, she brushed off the attention paid to her legs and glided into the restaurant.

"Hello, how are you doing today?" the greeter asked with a pleasant smile.

"Oh, nothing," Liyah said. "Do you perchance know if someone named Nicole has arrived yet? I'm supposed to meet her here."

"No, I don't think so." The greeter shrugged.

"Oh, ok. Could you get me a table for two, and guide her over here when she does?"

"Sure, ma'am. Just a moment."

"Figures she'd be late," she muttered to herself as the greeter guided her over to a table for two by the front. "At least I'll be able to see her coming from this spot."

She sat down in the chair pulled out for her, crossed her long legs and doffed her hat and sunglasses. Ordering a Corona with lime as she waited, she thought about how close they were growing up. Nicole, or "Nikki" always had this habit of being the wild one while Liyah was always the quiet one. Nonetheless, since they met each other back when they were eight in grade school, they were like siblings. Back then when Liyah was Omar, they were like Brother and Sister. "Now we're BOTH sisters," Liyah thought with a smirk.

Batting her almond-shaped eyes that were reflective of her Jamaican -Chinese roots, she looked out across the street to see Nikki coming, scrambling across the street. "Oh, there she is," Liyah said to no one as her beer arrived. "I hope she at least remembered her money."

Nikki walked into the restaurant fluffing her voluminous curly fro. Her large brown eyes sparkled as she looked for her friend. Her big silver earrings brushed against her shoulders as she turned her head to and fro looking for Liyah. "Bitch had BETTER be here..." Nikki had to admit that she really didn't know what to look for. It had been a few years since the last time she saw her childhood friend, and back then Liyah was Omar. She had only seen pictures of her friend as a girl but she knew pictures weren't always true to life. Nikki was the type to play things fast and loose with no worries, but she had to admit she was kind of nervous when she spotted the small-framed long haired beauty sitting close to the front of the restaurant. She adjusted her tight red wife beater fully aware that the puffy nipples of her breasts (the size of large oranges) were protruding and straining against the fabric. Her obscenely short denim skirt did nothing to hide her thick thighs as they hugged her round honey complexion ass. She walked over gingerly in her 80's style red pumps as her various bangles and jewelry jangled.

She stood behind Liyah and cleared her throat. Immediately her friend turned around and beamed. Nikki couldn't believe it. He...uh, she was downright beautiful. Her old friend Omar had always been the skinny kid and he hated it, but his small frame looked so natural as a woman. Long legs and torso, striking features. Liyah could be a model. Liyah stood up and hugged her friend tightly, "It's about time!"

"Oh please," Nikki said when they broke apart, "You know you probably just got here your damned self...look at you..." Nikki said holding her friend's arm up and away from her body to spin her around, "Is that why you call yourself 'Liyah'? Because you look like Aaliyah?" He reminded Nikki of like late singer Aaliyah in her prime, only Liyah had huge breasts, which had to be a strain on her nearly tiny frame. The pictures she saw of her friend did not do any justice. They must've been taken in the very beginning stages of Liyah's transformation.

Liyah shrugged as she sat down, "I took the hint from everyone who kept telling me I looked like her...so why not?"

Nikki laughed as she took a roll off of the table, "Omar...I mean *Liyah*..." she smiled, "This is crazy. I can't believe this..." she beamed. "You're gorgeous..."

"And look at you?" Liyah said blushing, "I see you went natural. I like you with big curly hair anyway."

Nikki played with her metal studded leather wristband, "Yeah my style has changed since high school."

"Yeah but I bet your ass is still wild as hell right?" Liyah said shaking her head.

"And you weren't but you gotta be now, damn how short are those shorts," Nikki said peering at her friends smooth long legs.

"So what are we doing today?"

"Relax, I got everything planned out okay?"

"I AM relaxed," Liyah said sipping her water looking around for their server. "What do you gotta do to get service around here?"

"No you're not relaxed, you think I'm gonna flake on you and make you pay for everything. Well HA!" Nikki playfully pointed at her friend. "I've got a real afternoon and evening planned and you won't have to worry about a thing."

"Okay," Liyah laughed, "Your mom's Mastercard?" she raised an eyebrow.

"No!" Nikki scoffed, "Give me some credit Liyah."

Liyah rolled her eyes, "Oh okay I'm sorry. We both know you have no credit."

Nikki laughed as she threw a napkin at the girl, "It's not my mom's!"

Liyah arched a brow.

"It belongs to my new sugar daddy." She pulled the plastic out of her purse and laid it on the table.

Liyah cracked up with laughter, "I knew it! Who is he this time?"

"Some art dealer in SoHo. Freakin' rich...he's older but he knows I do my thing."

"Umm hmmm," Liyah said skeptically, "I bet you do your thing alright."

"Yep, after this we're going to the spa, and then shopping, and then we are going to club all night long while being driven around. And today is going to be just like those commercials..."

"What?"

"Priceless." Nikki said giving a sly smile.

"Mmmhmm," Liyah said, rolling her eyes. "Sure honey. Just like the time I caught you trying to fuck the star of the guys AND girls basketball team back in high school."

"Please, girlfriend. You see homegirl was one of the stars of the women's final four this year, so hush!" Nikki said with a laugh as Liyah's beer arrived. "Besides, I'm a whole lot of woman for just one."

"So what about the dude?"

"Well, dude was hung like a star. I know you'd want a taste of something like that."

Liyah raised her eyebrows as she took a sip of the beer, then awkwardly paused as she set it down, looking for the right words to say. "So, where do you wanna start first with the shopping?"

"Well, thanks to my latest sugar daddy, I got some hookups at some exclusive boutiques down in SoHo. Stuff that only stars and people with money have..."

"And old money-chasing cum-guzzling sluts like yourself have," Liyah said, playfully sticking out her tongue before taking another sip of her beer. Nikki glared at Liyah, shaking her fluffy hair, "He's not "old-money". He's "Euro-trash soho art gallery dealer money". She snapped her fingers, "New money bitch. Get it right."

"Well, excuse me..." Liyah said snapping her fingers in return. "Should I start singing your favorite Prince song?"

"Yeah, yeah, yeah, I knew a girl named Nikki, yadda yadda yadda, sex fiend, blah blah blah," Nikki sang and they both laughed.

"Now, let's get something to eat. We have one hell of a day ahead of us. Waiter!" Nikki called out beckoning towards their server.

***

"So here it is," Nikki said, gesturing to the plain looking storefront. "I can tell by your reaction that you aren't impressed, but trust me, it's worth every penny."

Liyah looked at her friend, shrugged, then followed Nikki into the store. What the store lacked in ambiance, it more than made up for in clothes. It seemed like you couldn't swing a dead cat without finding a cute top or a nice skirt or a flattering pair of pants, and from the layout, swinging a dead cat would probably knock half the store over. The two old friends picked up handful after handful of new clothes, carefully avoiding the hipsters as they made their way through the aisles. A few of the customer's eyes lingered over the forms of the ladies, one catty female even rolling their eyes at the two.

The ladies made their way into the changing room, carelessly throwing their clothes onto the bench. Nikki had already tossed off her short skirt, and soon she was fluffing her large fluffy ringlets, posed in front of the mirror, swaying her hips from side to side as she showed off for herself.

"Hmm...let's see which of these clothes shows off my sexy body," Nikki seductively said as she bent over, letting her friend see her pantiless, hairless sex. "I know I wanna show it off."

"Yeah, I bet you do..." Liyah said trailing off, looking at the scene in front of her. "So, what do you wanna try on first?"

"Well, I think I wanna try these," Nikki said as she rummaged through the clothes there, digging out a pair of cream-colored capris that looked too narrow in the hips for her. "Let's see if this works..."

Nikki loosened up the belt on her skirt and tugged it down to the floor, showing her waxed-smooth sex in the mirror. She stepped into the pants easily, but struggled when it came time to pull them over her broad hips.

"O...I mean Liyah, could you help me with these?"

"Oh, sure," Liyah said as she walked over to pull the pants over her hips. Wrapping her fingers in the waist, she gave a good tug as Nikki jumped around, pulling both the pants onto her hips and Nikki's big soft ass onto her hips. She looked over her friend's shoulder at the mirror, looking at how those pants looked painted on her.

"Mmm...looks tasty there."

"Yeah, it is, if I say so myself," Nikki said with a mischievous smile. "They'd look nice on your legs too. Too bad your big dick couldn't fit in them," Nikki said, sticking her tongue out at the mirror.

"Ah, hush," Liyah said with a giggle, suppressing the embarrassment she felt as her tip started to push on the middle seem of her shorts.

Turning around towards her friend, Nikki giggled, "So, let's see what better living through chemistry can do for you!" She lifted up the shirt and saw Liyah's breasts encased in a simple black demi-bra, cupping what looked like a somewhat pendulous pair of breasts.

"Nice," Nikki said as she goosed them. "Kind of big for your frame. Where did you get them from?"

"Probably my mom," Liyah said. "It's the least she could have done after dying during my birth...give tits to her son," she continued, stifling a morbid giggle. Liyah, formerly known as Omar was raised solely by his father, breaking the stereotype that people like "her" had too much of a female influence in their lives.

"Well anyway, looks like you inherited some great ones."

"Yours aren't too shabby either," Liyah found herself saying. For some reason she couldn't look Nikki in the eye when she said this. She felt her shyness creeping back in the same way when she was a teenaged boy.

"You mean these?" said Nikki. She lifted up her tank top and pulled it off to reveal her not-too-big but not-too-small naturally bouncy breasts. Her nipples were all puffy. Liyah found her cock straining against her shorts.

"Touch them."

Liyah tried to laugh this off, "Oh, whatever Nikki."

"I'm serious, do you think they're firm enough? I'm thinking about buying some boobs..."

Liyah reached out and cupped the two nearly perfect caramel globes. She felt her breath catch in her chest. She hoped she could control her raging erection.

"Ooh, you're hands are soooo soft..." Nikki purred. Liyah gulped. Her wild friend oozed sensuality even when she wasn't trying. Liyah blushed.

"What?" Nikki said with a smirk on her face. "Why are you getting red in the face?"

"We've never ummm... I've never...you..." Liyah stuttered. She got caught up in the moment and began to relish the feel of the girl's hard nipples dragging against the center of her soft palms. They only seemed to get harder.

Nikki rolled her eyes, "We're both girls right?"

"Yeah but..."

"Girls who are gonna find some cute boys tonight," Nikki laughed as she pulled away from her friend to walk over to the entrance of the changing room.

"Yeah, about that..." Liyah said, confused. This was the second time Nikki made the allusion of her liking boys. Did Liyah think she was gay? Well technically she was because she was attracted to women. But did she ever think Omar was gay? Before Liyah could set her straight, Nikki was calling for the sales girl as she pulled back on her shirt.

"I want to try on this pink and black satin and lace corset with the black lace boyshorts with the ribbon trim?" She asked of the sales girl as she peeked out of the heavy curtain. "No I won't be needing help to put it on, my friend is here to help me," she turned and winked at Liyah.

Nikki handed her friend the lacy garments, then turned her back towards her as she cheesed for the mirror. "Could you help me slip this on?"

"Oh, sure," Nikki said. Liyah pulled the corset just tight enough to cling to Nikki's torso, then clumsily reached in front to pull off the wifebeater she was wearing underneath. As she pulled the shirt out of the corset, she managed to get a feel of her friend's puffy nipples, her hands lingering and tugging on them a bit. Her hands were wandering all over them just as she felt Nikki reach up and grab her arm, her lips cooing in her ear.

"LIYAH!" Nikki gasped as she playfully slapped her friend's hands away. "What are you doing?" she laughed.

Liyah smiled, "Oh nothing..."

"Ummm hmmm. Sure. Now pull that corset as tight as you can. Let's see how this looks."

Liyah wordlessly complied as she tugged at the laces, slowly bringing her friend's torso into shape. While Nikki was hardly wasp-thin, with such dramatic hips and thighs, her waist looked tiny in comparison. When she reached into the cleavage and hefted her breasts up a bit, she completed this classical looking image of beauty, all tits and ass and fertility and child support payments if a brother didn't act right. Nikki glanced up at her friend with a devilish smile, then started giggling a bit as she turned to Liyah.

"What?!"

"You know," Nikki said as she toed the panties on the floor. "I haven't seen how well you keep your feminine charms despite the, shall I say, masculine beginnings."

Liyah wrinkled her brow in thought, then said, "no..."

"C'mon, please?"

"I mean, since I transitioned, I mean..."

"Alright, alright. I'll even close my eyes. I know all women have their beauty secrets, especially when we aren't born beautiful," Nikki said, batting her eyelashes before making a show of squeezing the lids shut.

Liyah hesitated for a bit, then quickly shucked her shorts and jeans off in one stroke, her semi-hard dick flopping out in between. She looked at her friend's lips, feeling her shaft twitch a bit as she thought about being so bold as to stick the tip of her cock right on them. Her more shy sense getting the best of her, she thought herself calmer a bit before stepping into the panties and pulling them just above her knees. She pulled her dick firmly straight back, then nestled it in the crack of her ass, making her coo a bit as she reacted to the smooth skin-on-skin interaction. She quickly pulled the lacy underthings tight to her and took a look at herself in the mirror. A cute visage reflected back at her, especially the way the panties made her hips look bigger than they really were, and the cute camel toe that showed though, hiding her true sex.

"OK, you can open them now, Nikki."

"Nice, very nice!" Nikki said as she licked her lips. "Now turn around...le mme see that booty of yours..."

Nikki arched an eyebrow surprised. Her friend had one of the best asses she had ever seen. There was a dramatic dip in her lower back which curved out to a full and round shaped ass, even on the petite girl's body.

Nikki didn't think before she said, "If I didn't know any better, I'd rip those panties off and try to eat your pussy."

"Well," Liyah said, "You can still rip my panties off. I can give you something to taste."

Nikki gave her friend a curious look. Was Liyah serious? The whole situation had her instantly wet. She looked at this pretty girl who was packing major dick in those panties. What would it be like to fuck her?

"Well," Nikki said smiling, "It would be a real shame to rip those pretty panties. Why don't you just take them off?"

Skin flushing, Liyah did as she was told, her already erect dick springing forth.

Nikki licked her lips as she sat down in a nearby chair, her bosom pushed high by the restrictive corset. Liyah got hard watching her friend beckon her closer with her finger. She was so seductive.

Liyah walked forth with her hard veiny dick and Nikki immediately grabbed it. She was so horny right now. She ran her hands up and down the shaft and looked up into Liyah's eyes as she stroked it. She licked her full lips and slowly began to lick up and down her shaft, gingerly holding her friend's hard dick. Liyah hissed. This would be the first time since she'd been a woman that anyone had even touched her. It was hard to find lesbian girls who were into girls with built in dicks. It was hard to find ANYONE who would understand.

Who better to break her in than her best friend?

She fluttered her eyes open and looked down at Nikki as she licked the tip of her dick, her hand gently jacking the thick caramel log jutting out from her legs. She felt her nipples pebble up under her bra, making her draw in her breath sharply, as Nikki's afro bobbed slightly with her efforts. She started thinking about where she was, but there was just one thing she had to try first.

"Nikki," Liyah whispered nervously. "C-could you do me a favor?"

"I thought you were doing me one with that thick, luscious caramel candy you have here," Nikki said, sucking the tip before grabbing it and hitting it on the palm of her hand. "Are you sure you don't have implants? I mean, you can't be taking hormones with this."

"Nah...not with all the sleepless nights these puppies gave me when they came in," Liyah said. "Anyway, I know I've seen a lot of porn vids from the internet, and I just love to see a girl take it deep. I've always wanted to know what it feels like, but I've never had the chance. Could you..."

Liyah didn't get a chance to finish her sentence as Nikki took the tip into her dick into her mouth, swirling her tongue around before slowly inhaling her dick, inch by inch. As she worked her way down, she smiled and looked up into Liyah's eyes, even playfully giving her ass a smack. As she reached the midway point of Liyah's shaft, she started to hesitate a bit, and Liyah reached out as if to grab Nikki's afro, but stopped short.

Nikki reached up, grabbed Liyah's hand, wrapped it around her thick mane and nodded her head in assent. Liyah tugged on her friend's hair as Nikki guided her thick lips down that pulsing shaft, stopping only then her lips were flush with her friend's shaved base. She quickly pulled off of the meaty pole, gasping for breath between the giggles.

GIRL'S NIGHT OUT 2

"D amn, I didn't know you were so big! I never taken anything that big before, and especially that thick," Nikki gasped. "Wow!"

"Thanks, I think," Liyah said.

"Aww, don't be afraid," Nikki said as she bounced up, giving her friend a tight hug as her friend's dick bounced up between her legs. "It's alright," she continued with a peck on the cheek. "Now let's get dressed. I got more in store for you."

"Alright," Liyah said as she hunted for her shorts. "But just how am I supposed to fit in my shorts?"

"You aren't," Nikki said. "Could you loosen me up, please?" she said, offering her back to her friend.

"Uh, you seem to fail to realize that I don't live as Omar anymore. How would you react if you saw an Aaliyah look-alike with a bulge that belongs more on Lexington Steele? Who do you think I am? Ciara?"

"Well," Nikki said as she bent over in front of her friend. "I'd go like this..." she said as she grinded her ass on Liyah's cock, "just so I can tell my friends how hung their favorite songstress is... Now, quit your whining and pull on your shorts. I know just what to do."

As her friend did just that, Nikki grabbed up as many of the clothes in the dressing room as possible. She then leaned out and called for some help with all the clothes in her hands.

"I can't believe you're buying all that stuff without trying it on. Is dude that rich?" Liyah said as she zipped her shorts shut.

"In a word, yes. Now follow close."

Liyah followed her friend tightly, her nose pressed lightly into her afro. As they made their way out of the dressing room, Nikki made a point of dropping something a few times, making sure to bend over at the waist and make Liyah grimace from the sweet torture of her friend's ass. When they finally made it to the register, Nikki bent over in front of the counter to pass the bill with the credit card and grab the bags of clothes, all the while grinding on Liyah's denim-covered member. It got to the point where...

"Are you OK, ma'am?" the cashier said.

"Uh, yeah, yeah, I'm OK," Liyah nervously replied as she took a couple of bags from Nikki. "Just something from lunch bugging me, that's all."

As the transaction finally finished up, the two friends made their way out the store.

"Are you fucking nuts?!" Liyah quietly screamed at Nikki. "Your little stunt nearly got my secret revealed!"

"And what a lovely secret it is," Nikki said as she palmed the thick member through the shorts while giving her friend a peck on the cheek. "Now, let me show you where we're headed to next..."

Nikki and Liyah got into the waiting black car with all of their purchases in trendy shopping bags. As the driver pulled off, Liyah couldn't stop thinking about her sexy friend. She spied her smooth thick sexy thighs, exposed regardless of the best efforts of that tight denim skirt. She couldn't believe how good it felt to be deep throated like that. Her dick was bulging out of her shorts. She was so horny. She realized that their driver was only feet away behind a partition, but still she took this chance...

She unbuttoned her shorts, her thick caramel dick springing to life. Then as Nikki chattered mindlessly on her cellphone, she took her friend's free hand and guided it around her thick cock. Nikki looked over at her fully erect friend and just smiled. She was talking to her boyfriend as she slowly stroked the girl's cock up and down, "Yeah baby, I'm thinking of you too. Ummm hmmm. Yes..." She moaned. Liyah loved the sexy way her friend's voice sounded. Her eyes fluttered and she realized that the driver probably heard what was going on. His eyes locked with hers in the rearview mirror. Closing the partition would be too obvious, so Liyah just tried to sit tight.

Nikki began to aggressively stroke Liyah's thick veiny shaft as she spoke in kittenish tones on the phone to her "sugar daddy". It was bordering obscene, "Ummm hummm Daddy, and where do you want me to put it?"

Liyah had no idea what Nikki was talking about. It could've been a lamp or a painting in his apartment, but her tone of voice would cause any man to begin immediately jerking off. And as she stroked him, she knew Nikki was purposefully trying to get her more and more aroused. She got harder in her hand. Liyah threw her head back and moaned in a sexy way. The driver had a hard time keeping his eyes on the road. It was obvious he wanted to know what in the hell was going on back there.

Nikki began to stroke faster, and faster. Liyah felt like her whole body was on fire. She was already aroused from what they had done in that dressing room. It wouldn't be long until she would cum but...

"We're here," The driver announced as he pulled up right next to the spa.

"OK...I'll catch up with you tonight, or probably tomorrow, alright," Nikki said in a rush. Nikki breathed a sigh of relief as she stared at the thick member in her hand. "Damn that was close. I think I'm getting obsessed with your dick, and it's not a good thing."

"It's ok, babe, as long as I can get some fun too," Liyah said as she rubbed her fingers along Nikki's inner thigh. "Friends, OK?" she said before leaning in for a peck on the lips. Before she knew it, they were trying to suck the air out of each other, rubbing up on each other as Liyah eased her hand up under her friend's tight skirt, feeling her felt her soft pussy.

"OK, OK," Liyah said as she pushed her friend away, gasping for breath as she tucked her rapidly deflating dick back into her shorts. "You're my friend. Sorry...just got too carried away."

"Uh, yeah," Nikki said as she smoothed down her clothes, looking around at nothing in particular. "Driver...be available when I call, OK?"

"Yes, ma'am," the driver replied as both Nikki and Liyah slid out the back seat of the car and into the spa. Avoiding eye contact as much as possible, they walked into the spa, and almost ran into the front desk as they were trying awkwardly to avoid an awkward situation.

"Ladies," the tanned gentlemen said at the desk. "Are you here for your appointment now?"

"Uh, yes," Nikki said as she rifled through her purse and produced a sheet. "This is us right here."

***

After facials, massages and seaweed wraps, the girls sat together in a hot steamy sauna relaxing.

"Nikki, I really have to give it to you," Liyah said reclining with her eyes closed. "You really know how to treat a girl."

Nikki raised an eyebrow, "Give it to me?"

Liyah laughed, the sexual tension had been building all day between them. They were trying to avoid their lust for each other but it seemed inevitable. "What are you talking about?"

"You said you really have to 'give it to me'. So..."

"And I also said you really know how to treat a girl."

Nikki smirked, "I think you're right..."

Before Liyah knew it Nikki was before her in the steamy sauna on her knees. She had moved her friend's towel out of the way and began to handle her hard veiny caramel flavored stick. Liyah gasped, remembering how her friend had deep throated her earlier in the changing room at the boutique.

Nikki began to languidly lick her friend's tip, making Liyah's nipples harden. By now her towel had completely fallen away, and her large breasts and hard nipples were exposed to the moist and humid air.

Nikki licked the sides of Liyah's shaft as Liyah tweaked her own hard nipples. This is what she had been waiting for all day long.

"This is kind of hot," Nikki said, "Me sucking my 'homegirl's' dick," she looked up from beneath her messy curls and smiled as she flicked her tongue feather like all up and down the underside of Liyah's shaft.

"Ummmm..." Liyah said biting her bottom lip, "hot indeed..."

Nikki slowly slid down her friend's dick, taking her in inch by inch. Liyah was beside herself moaning loudly, hoping no one in the spa heard them. It was quite dangerous the way they lost control. Anyone could come in and discover them at any moment. This only added to their lusty feelings.

Liyah felt her tip lodged inside Nikki's throat. The girl was skilled. She slurped around Liyah's hard cock, massaging the girl with her throat muscles and lips and tongue.

"Oh shit..." Liyah moaned deeply, grabbing a fistful of her friend's hair.

Nikki eventually came up for air, though slowly, inching her mouth up Liyah's shaft, leaving a trail of saliva.

"Damn it Nikki," Liyah huffed.

"Damn it what?"

Liyah couldn't even talk. Nikki had turned her into a blubbering mess. Nikki began to bob up and down on her hardness, slobbering and slurping as she moaned, "you taste so good Liyah..."

Liyah bit her bottom lip and curled her toes as Nikki concentrated on her tip, licking and sucking and spitting it back out again. She made an absolute mess.

"You're so fucking nasty girl," Liyah groaned.

"Umm hmm..." is all Nikki could get out.

Nikki bobbed up and down faster and faster on her friend's dick, slick with spit. Liyah felt a building sensation deep in her gut. "Oh shit, Nikki, you're going to make me cum..."

Nikki continued to suck her dick, jacking it with her mouth.

"Oh shit Nikki..."

Nikki pulled up still holding Liyah's cock, rapidly jerking it with her hands until white creamy jizz spurted from the tip.

"Oh God yes!" Liyah cried out after cumming the hardest she's ever come in a long time. Nikki moaned and rubbed her friend's cum all over her friend's cock, licking her lips.

Liyah panted as she came down from her high, "I forgot how nasty you were."

"Well now do you remember?"

"Definitely."

* * *

After their session in the sauna, Liyah and Nikki showered and headed to the spa's salon. They both got their hair done, turning down the option of being made up since they had hours before they'd be hitting the town that night. While Nikki got the curl pulled and pressed straight out of her hair, Liyah's was set in big bouncy waves.

Soon they were back in the black car again, headed back to the apartment Nikki shared with her boyfriend. Nikki turned toward her friend, flipping her hair, "So, what do you think? A quick nap before dinner and then the club?"

"Sure," Liyah said, noticing how pretty her friend was. When her hair was straight, her natural auburn color showed more and glinted in the light. It was cut bluntly at the ends, right past her shoulders. "Yeah, I guess I'm beat too."

Nikki smiled, "You sure are. I made sure of that didn't I?"

Liyah blushed.

"You're so cute when you blush. You know you really make a beautiful woman."

Liyah blushed even more, "Nikki, come on knock it off..."

"Yeah I'm sorry," Nikki shrugged as they pulled up in front of her apartment building. She gave the driver some instructions for later and then the girls brushed past the doorman right up to Nikki's loft.

"So this is the place, huh?" Liyah said as the elevator lurched to a stop.

"Yep, this is it."

As Nikki opened up the elevator door, Liyah walked in and took a good look at the place. The apartment seemed almost cavernous, with the effect enhanced by the huge windows on one side of the apartment and the low-slung furniture. Tiptoeing carefully, she tossed the bags of clothes onto the red and white leather couch, then walked around it and took a seat, sinking in as she put her feet up on the table.

"Hey Liyah!" Nikki called out from the kitchen. "What do you want to drink?"

"I-I guess something from the liquor cabinet. What do you have?"

"Well, I have some Cristal champagne, not that Cristal you got for us back in high school."

"Hey, what did I know? I was 15 and trying to be like Jay-Z! Besides, that liquor clerk lied to me," Liyah giggled. "Just gimme some."

"OK," Nikki said as she reached under the bar and pulled out two bottle of champagne, showing the bottles before walking. "Cristal it is. And be careful what you say...you may be giving me some before the night is done."

"Yeah, yeah. You've been obsessed with my dick all day. Give it a rest, ma!" Liyah said as she took the bottle from Nikki's hand. "Besides, we gotta save some energy for the club."

"Yeah, you have a point," Nikki said as she opened up her bottle, then moved to open her friend's. "What do you plan on wearing?"

"I dunno. I guess I can look through this stuff and figure something out. By the way, where are the glasses for this?"

Liyah looked up to see Nikki sipping champagne right out the bottle. "Guess that answers my question," Liyah said as she laughed.

"Who needs glasses? You know how I like to take is straight to the head..." Nikki gave a sly sneer as she tossed the bottle up to her lips, rivulets of champagne streaming down her neck in gluttony.

"Alright," Liyah said, almost not able to concentrate as she watched the throat muscles in her friend's neck work that champagne down. Liyah took a huge swig from the bottle, downing almost a third of it as she felt it fizz in her throat. The champagne had an effect immediately, giving her a nice pleasant buzz. She sat back and nursed the rest of the bottle, looking at her friend as she did likewise. As the alcohol started to take effect, her mind started to wander. What does she look like naked? Is that pussy as good as it looks? Is it tasty? How does it taste? Could Liyah reveal the fact that she's still a virgin?

She looked over at her friend, who was sipping her champagne in the same way, her eyes wandering over her curves and down in between her legs. She wondered how those juicy tits would look and how suckable they would be in her mouth. Sipping the champagne, she got an idea that would allow her a chance to check out her friend's dangerous curves.

"Nikki," Liyah said as she managed to suppress a burp, "wanna try on some of these clothes? I wanna see what you wanna go to the club in." Liyah leaned over to look through the bags of clothes to see what she would like to see her friend in when she felt fingertips brushing along her arm.

"Don't you worry, Liyah. I got something upstairs that guaranteed to make every dick hard in the club, and I do mean," she said looking right down at Liyah's crotch, "Every. Dick."

Nikki walked away with her friend with a strut, wiggling those hips as she made her way out the living room and up the spiral staircase to the bedroom. Liyah sat there nervous and a bit horny, feeling her nipples harden under her shirt and feeling thankful for the numbing of her nerves the alcohol produced. Her mind started wandering in the dead quiet of the loft, thinking about what she wanted to do to her friend. But wait? She didn't want to take her, did she? After all, she chose to live as a girl, and girls don't do that, right? Even though she had been a guy whose transformed into a girl, her attraction for women remained static. The fact that technically she was also a virgin didn't help her confusion either. What would she do if given the chance?

She was this close to drifting off to sleep when the metal clang of the spiral stairs woke her up. By the time she got her bearing, she looked up at the sex goddess in front of her. The first thing she noticed was how much taller she was...and with calf-length red patent length lace-up boots with six-inch platform heels, she couldn't help but be a little bit taller than her friend. Her hips seemed poured into a matching skirt that didn't have enough hip or length to keep those thighs and that ass in check. The long, soft torso nipped in for a tiny waist before spreading up and out for the tiny red patent leather top whose laced seemed to force her cleavage out more than contain it, with her flesh looking to burst out of every seam. To cap it off, Nikki wore this fire engine red lip gloss that seemed to reflect how wet she could be between her legs and had Liyah thinking about yet another go round with those lips and her...

"Do you like?"

Liyah simply nodded her head, then fell out laughing rolling over the couch.

"Gee," Nikki said, "You know how to boost a chick's confidence."

"No, it's fine," Liyah said. "Perfect, in fact."

"Why don't you look and see if there's something nice you want to put on, Liyah?"

Liyah thought to herself, then started rustling through the bags of clothes. She had trouble finding what she was looking for, but when she found it, she snatched it out of her bag and hid it behind her.

"Hey, what was that you pulled out?"

"Don't worry, Nikki. You'll see in a bit," Liyah said with a wink as she awkwardly backed away from her, then switched it in front of her as she worked her way over and up the stairs to Nikki's bedroom. Once she reached the bedroom, she closed the door and tossed the dress on the low-slung bed. She gently lifted her shirt over her head, careful not to mess up her perfectly coifed hair, then shucked off her shorts.

Looking over in the mirror, Liyah lightly touched her hair, then checked out her body. "Mmm, if I weren't me, I'd love to fuck me," Liyah thought to herself. With one very notable exception, she'd successfully made herself into her dream woman. Feeling her dick pulse in her panties, she tugged at the bra straps to heft her boobs up a bit. Picking up the black spaghetti-strapped dress, she held it to her form, then realized that she'd had to lose the bra for the dress to work. She looked at her shoes, noting that they were probably wrong for the outfit, but shrugged as she stepped into the dress and pulled it up her body.

As the dress went up, it seemed to cling to every single curve she had, which was exactly what she was intending. After pulling up her breasts to give herself some cleavage, she thought of the perfect way to tease her friend. With that in mind, she reached under the dress and pulled her panties off in one swipe letting her semi-hard dick press firmly against the tight fabric.

The effect complete, she opened the door to the bedroom and called out, "Nikki, are you ready?"

"Yeah girl! What are you wearing?"

"Just close your eyes, and you'll see in a bit."

Satisfied that her friend's eyes were closed, she walked nervously down the stairs. She stroked herself through the dress one last time, put her hands to the side.

"You can open your eyes Nikki."

Nikki turned around and looked at her Liyah. A look of surprise and lust came over her face as she licked her lips. "Someone forgot to tuck huh?"

"Nope."

Liyah smiled, "Good to know," Then she leaned back and looked at the overflowing cleavage and the way the dress simply clung to her hips. But all that just led to one thing in her mind.

"I never thought a dick would look so sexy on a chick until I saw you naked," Nikki said as she crawled over the couch to her friend. "In fact, I think it makes it even sexier, if that makes sense." Nikki walked over to Liyah and pawed at her dick while looking up and kissing her friend on the lips, intertwining their tongues in the process.

Suddenly, Liyah pushed her friend away from her, then bent her over the couch and kneeled behind Nikki. She lifted up the tiny skirt and smacked the juicy ass that was presented to her. Grateful that her friend went pantiless, Liyah decided to dive right for Nikki's pussy, tonguing it in long strokes.

Nikki's eyes rolled up into her head as she gasped and moan, "Oh God, yes...lick me Liyah..."

Liyah traced her tongue along her friend's slit, then languidly swirled her tongue around her friend's hard protruding clit. Her dick became harder and harder inside of her dress as she listened to her friend moan and felt her squirm with pleasure. The louder Nikki got, the more ravenous Liyah became. Liyah slid her tongue into Nikki's pussy deep, deep until her face nuzzled between those plump firm ass cheeks.

Nikki arched her back and screamed, "Fuck me with your tongue Liyah! Yes!"

Liyah rubbed her face in Nikki's ass as she fucked her with her tongue, massaging her inner walls with it.

Before they both knew it Nikki was coming hard onto Liyah's face.

GIRL'S NIGHT OUT 3

Nikki whimpered after her orgasm but she was clearly ready for more, "Put that hard dick in me baby. Make me cum all over it."

Liyah was rock hard and ready to go. She lifted her dress up over her hips and grabbed her cock, wanting so badly to feel those tight wet sugar walls coddle it and massage it to the point of ecstasy. But before she did anything she thought about her pending virginity. Should she tell Nikki that she's never fucked anything before except her precious juicy mouth today? If she didn't say anything, would Nikki forgive her for coming too fast? It was her first piece of ass and it was oh so luscious. She knew she wouldn't last long.

Liyah shrugged it off and decided that saying anything would ruin the moment. She decided to dive in, literally. She lined up her dick with Nikki's pussy, then tried to push herself in. After Nikki guided her into her slick pussy, Liyah just grabbed Nikki's ass and started pounding away. Somehow, she had fell over into the couch, almost burying Nikki into the couch, but she kept fucking into that wet, slick channel, shaking as she felt her hard nips graze Nikki's back. She brushed her bouncy curls out of her face, then pulled on her friend's hair.

"You ready for me to cum, bitch!"

"Fuck yeah Omar...I mean Liyah! Nut in my pussy you studly bitch!" Nikki gritted through her teeth.

Suddenly, Liyah felt her dick explode inside of Nikki, soaking her pussy. Liyah felt like she was peeing but it was just so much cum. She felt like she was squeezing her very self out of that little hole at the end of her member, huffing and puffing as she finally felt the sweat on her face. Leaning back a little she could see her own cum drip nastily out of her friends open and swollen pussy. She slowly calmed down, coming to rest on top of her friend, her breasts seeming huge as they pressed on her friend's back.

"Whew! That was fun," Liyah said. "Still wanna go to the club?"

"I think we're already there," Nikki said. "Or more like the club was in me. Damn, if I knew you were like that, I would have fucked you years ago!"

Brushing back her friend's hair, Liyah said, "but if we did, we wouldn't have been friends."

"True."

"Dame besos, mamacita," Liyah said before leaning into a long kiss, slipping out of her friend as their tongues wrapped up in each other.

They both knew this was going to be the beginning of something good.

***

The End.

TRANNY ENCOUNTERS - ESCORT FUCKED

W alking out into the parking lot, I wiped the sweat off my face as I headed to the car. Though it was spring time, the temperature seemed to be rising in Bluehaven fast. Atleast classes for the day were over and I could go home and relax in a nice bath. Just as I sat down in the car, my phone began to buzz.

"Hello, Simone," said a familiar female voice.

"Hello Cherrie," I replied.

"How are you today?" she asked, being polite.

"Good..." I responded.

"Are you free tonight?" asked Cherrie.

I bit my lip as I knew the question was coming. Money had been really tight. Ever since my parents had died it had been really difficult to hold down a steady job and do community college. A girl at college had introduced me to Cherrie who had the answers to my problems. Cherrie ran a very high class escort agency in Bluehaven. It was very hush-hush. Her clientele included some really big names ranging from big shot business-men to high profile celebrities.

"Do you have a client for me?" I asked.

"Yes, it's a 3 hour appointment," she informed me.

"Who's the client?" I asked.

"Well, I don't know. The job is coming through a referral. Usually I would not agree to something like this, but the middle man is someone I know personally and a very old client. So I had to consider it."

"What does this client want?" I asked.

"I was told that this particular client wants someone young, between the age of 20-25, blonde, supple breasts and willing to do anything. So, natu-rally, I thought of you."

"Cherrie, I don't know. Have you even met this client?"

"No."

"Then how can I just go to client that even you haven't met and vetted."

"It pays more than what you would usually get for a full night."

"How much more?" I asked.

"Two thousand."

I was a bit shocked when I heard the figure. Usually most of the regulars I saw only wanted my company for a couple of hours and it wasn't half the price of what was being offered right now. This was over double and quite enticing.

"Simone?"

"Yes, Cherrie. I'm here," I replied.

"Well, are you interested or not?" she asked.

I silently sat in my seat, staring at the steering wheel, thinking if I should accept this offer.

"Simone, you need to answer me. Otherwise, I need to try to get a hold of one of the other girls."

"I'm still thinking..." I replied.

"Think faster, I need an answer before I hang up on this call," she said sounding a little annoyed.

The money was good. More than I had ever received for anything I had done.

"Simone!"

"Umm, sorry... uhh... yeah I'm free tonight," I replied.

"Good. So..." I cut her off.

"But... I have some conditions," I said, trying to sound a bit authoritative.

"And what are these conditions?" she asked sounding even more annoyed than before.

"No whips, no chains, no pain of any kind, no golden showers, no anal and absolutely no marks," I said. "The last client you booked me with wanted it all and it was not pleasant."

"Darling, in this business you cant keep conditions. The client pays you and you do what the client wants. End of story."

"Then I'm out," I said. I had heard the whole give the client what he wants speech before. While not every client was the same, there was an occasional one who didn't care and pretty much took what they wanted, leaving girls like me with bad experiences. And even though Cherrie said she would get another girl, I knew she didn't really have any options to go with. Most girls would never go out on something like this blind and she obviously didn't have any choice but to come to me.

There was silence on the line for a few moments. Maybe my bluff didn't work.

"Fine," she said, sighing into the phone.

"Okay. I'll do it then."

"You are to go to the Hotel Marquis. At the reception, ask if they have something for you. You will be handed an envelope with further instructions. Be there by 9pm and don't be late."

"Fine."

"Oh and another thing, the client has a request."

"Which is...."

"Dress classy."

"Don't I always?" I said, agitated.

"Classy doesn't always mean sexy. This client is apparently very particular and clear that you dress a bit conservative, but sexy."

"Okay, got it."

"Good, don't be late," she said before hanging up.

A little exasperated, I was glad the call had ended. Though I had nothing against Cherrie, she could be quite cold at times. She was very moody. On certain days, she would be like the best friend you never had. On others, she behaved like the ice queen.

Putting my phone back in my purse, I drove home. Fifteen minutes later, I took care of some college work before I made some dinner and left for my very secretive appointment for the night. Unfortunately, the college work kept me going through most of evening so I didn't time to prepare dinner at all. I only had time for a sandwich and a soda.

By 7:30, I got into the tub and took a nice warm bath with some scented oils. The day at college had been a bit rough, plus the heat did not help at all. I didn't want to meet a client smelling disgusting. After I was done, I decided not to use a lot of make and to keep things a little more simple. I never did usually use a lot of make-up, but tonight I decided that I didn't need to go all out to impress the client either.

After make-up and hair, I picked out a lace bra with matching panties, garters, and some black nylon stockings. I decided to go with a red dress that looked conservative enough to appease the client. Putting on a pair of black 4 inch pumps, I gave myself a once over before I decided to leave.

As I headed downstairs, I almost grabbed my keys but stopped. Maybe going out dressed to the nines to an elegant hotel in a shitty Honda Civic wasn't the best idea. I called a cab.

By 9pm, I was at the Hotel Marquis, heading toward the lobby. There was an older woman, probably mid-forties, standing behind the counter as I arrived at the desk.

"Do you have something for Simone Bradley?" I asked.

The woman looked in my direction and raised her eyebrow. She obviously knew why I was here.

"One moment please," she said, turning and walking away.

She returned a minute later with an envelope and handed it over to me.

"Thanks," I said and walking away from the desk.

Opening the envelope, I pulled out a key card and a note.

ROOM 704

Apart from the room number there was nothing else written on the piece of paper. Discarding the note and the envelope, I headed toward the elevator. Moments later, I stood outside Room 704 with the key card in my hand.

Taking a deep breath, I unlocked the door and let myself inside.

The room was mostly dark with just a couple of lights on. It looked as if no one was inside.

"Hello?" I called out nervously.

"Take off your dress," said a female voice.

Still nervous, I put my purse on the table and unzipped my dress, letting it fall on the floor.

"Did you agent give you the details for tonight?" asked the female voice.

I nodded, "Yes."

"And was it specified that you will be willing to do whatever the client asks of you, even if its unorthodox?" asked the female voice.

I nodded again. "Yes."

A light turned on next to the couch where a woman sat with her legs crossed. She had red hair, alabaster skin, and was wearing a white silk top and a black skirt. She looked very elegant, and with the look that she was giving me, she looked like the no nonsense type. Getting up she walked over and stood right in front of me. I noticed she had piercing green eyes as she looked me up and down.

"When does my client get here?" I asked.

Folding her hands, she gave me a sheepish grin. "I am the client."

This was definitely a first for me. Though I had been with a couple once, I had never been with a woman one on one.

Moving to a chair close by, she took a seat and crossed her legs, like a well-mannered woman would.

I stood there nervously as I didn't know what to expect.

"Take off your bra," she said, authoritatively.

Taking a deep breath, I began to unclasp my bra.

"Slowly," she ordered.

I unclasped my bra and slowly slid the straps down. Making eye contact with her, I dropped it on the floor. Running my hand on my breasts, I tried to cover them up.

"Don't do that," she said.

I immediately stopped and put my hands to my sides.

"Take your panties off; you can keep the garters and stockings on though."

Obeying once again, I pulled my panties down and dropped them on the floor next to my bra.

"Take off your shoes, I want you comfortable."

Slipping off my shoes, I stood in front of her, my hands a little fidgety as I felt like I was on display.

"Get on your knees in front of me."

Again, I did as I was told as I moved up next to her and got on my knees. She picked up a white box on the stand next to her and handed it to me.

"Open it and remove what's inside."

I opened the box and pulled out a white collar with a ring in the middle and a leash that could be attached to it.

"Let me help you with that," she cooed.

Handing the items to her, I lifted my hair as she put the collar around my neck and then attached the leash to it.

Leaning down, she gave me a soft, gentle kiss on the lips. "You're mine now."

Uncrossing her legs, she pulled her skirt up. As she did so, I noticed the garters, stockings, and the pair of silky black panties. The panties were covering a huge bulge. I gulped and looked up at her as she gave me a devilish grin.

"Take my panties off."

Doing as I was told, I pulled her panties off and a big cock sprang up from between her legs.

I gasped as her huge cock saluted me. It looked like it was close to 10 inches. I looked up at her even more nervous than before.

"Is this your first time with a woman with a cock?" she asked.

I nodded.

"Good! That's what I wanted," she said with a smile, pulling the leash toward her big meat stick. "Lick it."

I moved my hand up, grabbed her rock-hard shaft, and slowly began to lick it.

"Did I ask you to use your hands?" she growled.

"No... no..," I responded meekly.

"No what?" she asked menacingly.

"No, ma'am," I replied.

"Good," she said, her face lightening up a little.

Putting my arms to my sides, I began to lick her shaft from root to tip.

A moan escaped her lips as I licked the tip.

"You can take it inside your mouth," she whispered.

Slowly, without moving my hands, I took the head of her cock into my mouth. Lowering my head slowly, I tried to take in as much as I could. Due to the sheer size and girth of the thing, I was only able to take it midway and then slowly began to bob up and down on it.

"Good girl."

Pulling her cock out of my mouth, she grabbed my chin and gave me another soft kiss.

"My cock tastes good... doesn't it?"

"Mmhmm," I nodded.

"You want more?"

I nodded again.

"Then come suck on it some more," she said as she stood up.

She held her cock and gave it a few tugs before I took it back into my mouth. She grabbed my head and forced her cock further down my throat as she held on to the leash.

"Mmm, yeah, that's it. Suck on my dick."

I gave her cock a few licks and took it down and bobbed my head on it a few times and repeated these motions several times. Her moans and groans told me I was doing a pretty good job of blowing her.

"Look up at me when you do that," she grunted.

Making eye contact, I sucked the head back inside my mouth.

"Good girl. Keep sucking."

And I did.

Dropping the leash, she grabbed my head with both her hands and began to force fuck my face, pushing her cock deeper down my throat, causing me to gag. I held on to both her legs for support as she roughly fucked my mouth.

Holding me in place with three-fourths of her cock inside my mouth, she leaned down and spanked my ass. A few seconds later, she let me come up for air as she pulled it out. A sting of saliva connected my lips with her cock. Grabbing it, she began to slap my face.

"You like that? You like how I force fuck your face?"

I could only squeal in reply as she kept slapping me with her cock.

"Take more," she said, grabbing my hair and pushing her cock back into my mouth.

This went on for a few more minutes before she decided to pull out and let me catch my breath.

"Move into the bedroom, on your hands and knees."

Obeying her command, I got on my hands and knees as she led me to the bedroom.

"Get on the bed! On your hands and knees!" she ordered.

I moved into doggy position with my ass and pussy on display before her.

"Mmm, look at that pretty pink pussy," she said, rubbing my pussy.

I moaned as I felt her fingers rub my clit. A few seconds later, I felt a finger probe my pussy. She began to slowly move her finger in and out. I moaned in pleasure as she began to increase her speed. I felt my orgasm begin to rise.

"Ask for permission," she said, continuing to finger me.

"May I please cum," I squealed.

"You may," she replied and began to finger me faster.

Just seconds later, my orgasm hit as I felt my body begin to shake and quiver. As my orgasm died down, she removed her finger and flipped me over.

"What do you say?" she asked, pulling the leash.

"Thank you," I replied.

"Good girl."

Leaning down, she kissed me once again. This time a little more passionately. I was surprised at how soft her lips really were. Earlier I couldn't tell as she would just give me a peck on the lips and pull away. It didn't take long for me to being returning her kisses as we began to furiously make out.

"On your hands and knees again," she whispered silently as she broke the kiss.

Once in position, she aimed her cock at my pussy and slowly began to push in. I winced as she entered me deeper and deeper. I had never had a dick this big and thick before as I felt my pussy tightly grip her beast. Once down to the hilt, I buried my face into the mattress as she held me in place. After a few seconds, she began to push in and pull out.

"Push back on my cock," she commanded.

I did as I was told and began to bounce back and forth on her cock. She leaned down and grabbed the leash and began to pull on it as I fucked myself on her cock.

"You like that, slut?"

"Oohh yes."

"You like taking my big fat she-cock?"

" Oh yes, I love it!" I exclaimed.

"That's what I like to hear. Keep bouncing on that dick, slut."

A few bounces later, she pulled out. Grabbing my head, she pulled me off the bed and pushed me against the glass window of the bedroom.

Pulling my ass cheeks apart, she drove her mammoth beast right back inside my dripping wet pussy.

"That's it, slut. Scream for me. I want noise complaints. I want security to show up at the door so I can answer the door with your juices dripping off my big, thick cock!"

"FUCK FUCK FUCK!" I groaned as she drilled me hard and fast.

She pulled my right leg up and began to fuck me like there was no tomorrow as I leaned back a bit and grabbed on to her neck for dear life. Guessing that this position was a little uncomfortable, she put my leg back down as I arched my back. She grabbed on to my hips and kept pounding me.

"That's it! Take that dick!"

All it took was a few more strokes and my orgasm hit me again. This time my orgasm hit me even harder as I got pounded like a cheap whore.

"You didn't ask for permission!" she growled and began to spank my ass really hard as she pounded me. It hurt and stung like hell but I didn't care as I rode my orgasm in complete ecstasy. Just as I finished, she pulled her cock out of me and forced me to the floor.

Grabbing my hair she began to jerk off on my face. All it took was a few pumps and I felt rope after roper of cum hit my face. It felt warm, and it felt heavy as some of it flew into my hair, some hit my nose and my chin. Once she was done, she released my hair as I fell back against the bed.

As she pulled me up on my feet, I almost fell back as my legs felt like jelly. Once on my feet, she pulled me close to her and kissed me again.

"You can stay the night if you wish," she whispered.

"I can't."

"As you wish," she said, moving back.

She opened a drawer on the nightstand beside the bed and handed me an envelope.

"Take a shower before you leave," she ordered.

I complied.

Once I was done, I dressed up and caught a cab home. The entire ride back, I kept rethinking the whole night as my pussy began to leak again.

A simple request

"So, you are completely aware when you're in wolf-mode, right?"

Lucas' voice came out a little shakier than he intended, but it wasn't out of fear. It was out of anticipation for what he was about to ask his boyfriend to do for the first time in their two-year-long relationship.

Jace huffed in laughter. "Yeah. I've told you before: It's all me. With a weird urge to just haul ass in no particular direction through the woods all night."

They were hanging out on his bed, cuddling and just quietly enjoying each other's company while a playlist of indie rock played from Lucas' open laptop.

Lucas was laid on top of his boyfriend's broad chest, content as Jace ran a large hand through his hair. He had broken the silence between them with his question seemingly out of nowhere. Not really though. The idea had been on his mind for a long time.

"I wouldn't be taking advantage of you then," he murmured.

"What?"

"I want you to fuck me while you're turned."

There was no answer right away, as Lucas suspected. He looked up at Jace and was met with a wordless, wide-eyed gaze.

He sucked in a breath, feeling the heat of embarrassment rushing into his face. "I'm sorry. Did I cross a line? I know it's really weird. You don't have to—"

"No!" Jace interjected. "No, babe. I'm into it. Super into it. Just surprised me."

Lucas sighed in relief. "So...you'll do it?"

"Yeah. I mean, as long as you're absolutely sure about it."

"Very sure," Lucas said. "I've been thinking about it since the first time I saw you like that."

Jace gave an inquisitive hum. "Oh?"

Lucas had certainly jerked off to the thought more than once. It had surprised him when his fantasy shifted to it one night, but he had never cum so hard in his life until then. He wanted this so bad. His cock twitched in interest from the thought of it.

"Yeah." Lucas paused, swallowing hard. "Just...being on all fours with your huge weight on me, pounding me hard and fast into the mattress like a wild animal."

"You want me to mount you?" Jace's heartbeat had started to thunder.

Lucas nodded. "And do you guys knot? Like dogs?"

"Yeah," Jace said after clearing his throat which did nothing to help the huskiness that had settled into it. "There's...there's always a lot of cum too."

Lucas groaned, rubbing his growing erection against Jace's hip. "I wanna know how it feels."

"Fuck," Jace hissed, finally removing his hands from where they had been tightly gripping Lucas' tank top to roughly grab his ass. "I'll do it. I'll do it, babe."

Lucas let his hand explore under Jace's shirt, deciding the rest of this conversation could happen later. "We can talk about specifics tomorrow."

"Good. Because you've gone and got me rock hard right now—take care of it."

"Ass," Lucas said, smirking.

"Well, seeing as you've offered..."

~*~

The next week during the full moon found Lucas in the same place. He had been prepping himself for a while, working through various increasing sizes of dildos until he was fucking himself slow and deep on the one Jace swore was closest to his wolf form's size. It was massive.

Lucas continued to neglect his dick, not wanting to cum before the big show. He hoped Jace would show up soon because he was absolutely throbbing and desperate at that point, shaking with nerves and the need to be filled with werewolf cock.

He shuddered in anticipation at the telltale scratching below the open window that signified his boyfriend's arrival.

Jace's massive bulk blocked the bright moonlight from illuminating the room for a moment as he slunk in. He stood at the foot of the bed, breathing heavily as Lucas made a show of moaning and fucking himself open. His dark fur glistened and rippled over powerful muscles, and his bright golden gaze seemed feral and covetous. He growled lowly, possessively baring his large fangs. He was looking to claim.

Lucas' eyes strayed downwards, watching as the werewolf's huge cock unsheathed and filled. He sucked in a breath, clenching around the dildo at the sight of it already swelling a little at the base. God, he was so ready for that knot—and all that cum, and that deep pounding. Oh, fuck was he ever ready.

Whining, he slowly removed the dildo, tossing it aside. He shakily got up on his knees and turned, lowering to all fours and presenting his lubed-up, stretched-open hole. He felt the ring of muscle twitch and heard Jace groan roughly.

The mattress dipped with a sudden weight, and Lucas gasped as he felt two big, hairy hands grab his ass with zero trepidation. They squeezed once before pulling his cheeks apart. Jace's claws didn't break the skin but pressed hard enough into the meat of Lucas' skin to make themselves known. Just one hasty move would be enough to draw blood.

Lucas felt a hot, humid breath panting against his junk and backside. Before he was able to process anything, Jace's wide, flat tongue licked a slow stripe up his taint and over his hole. Jace; always an ass man in any form. Lucas didn't mind indulging his boyfriend. Not one bit. He shivered, letting out a pitiful whimper and rocking back against the canine snout.

From there, Jace set about a languid pace, not going beyond teasing him, refusing to have his tongue delve inside. It was just enough to keep Lucas away from the edge, keeping him horny and wanting more. It was maddening.

After an agonizing while, Jace abandoned this to lap at Lucas' balls and give quick little wet flicks of his tongue along his aching shaft. What sounded close to a deep chuckle rumbled through his chest as Lucas' soft moans became impatient. Enough indulging.

Lucas meant to spout a witty reprimand to tell his boyfriend to just get on with it, but his pleasure-addled brain could only think to let two breathy, needy words pass his lips.

"Fuck...me."

Finally, he felt the thick head of his boyfriend's huge wolf cock, slick with precum, probing against his loose entrance. Lucas had to refrain from bucking his hips back and just taking the whole damn thing in one motion. Even he had the mind to know it would have to be slow at first. He didn't have to like it though.

He took each inch like a goddamn champ until Jace was seated fully inside of him. They took a moment, letting Lucas get accustomed to it. It was so much better than the dildo. Just the heat of it turned him on so much, feeling it throb against his walls.

Jace was shaking, already panting in Lucas' ear, hips twitching now and then as if his control was hanging by a thread.

Now. Lucas needed Jace to move now. As if reading his mind, Jace pulled back slowly before starting up a moderate thrust. The stretch was magnificent. With Jace's girth and length, it was impossible for Lucas' prostate to not be assaulted with every motion. Each thrust was punctuated by Lucas' loud, unrestrained moans which quickly egged Jace onto building to a brutal pace.

Yes. Yes, yes, yes. This is was Lucas had been dying for. Normally, he would be a lot more involved when he and his boyfriend fucked, moving back to meet his thrusts. But, now he was completely immobilized by pleasure underneath Jace's weight. He had dropped onto his elbows, ass-up, unable to hold himself up anymore as Jace bared down on him.

Lucas could see Jace's hands in his peripheral, one on either side of his head as his boyfriend braced his arms for leverage, slamming into him again and again. Feral growls and snarls sounded above him, and he could even feel a few drops of thick saliva falling onto the back of his neck and shoulders.

Lucas' cock bounced hard, hot and heavy underneath him. He hadn't even touched it, but he knew it was about ready to blow just from the rough pounding. The absolute monster inside of him stirring up his guts was bringing him rapidly towards orgasm. His chest heaved as intense pleasure raced under his skin.

He thought he might pass out before it all came to a head, but then he was suddenly cumming with a broken cry. He clenched hard around Jace, practically screaming as his dick pumped out a massive amount of cum. Drops of it splattered everywhere as he was brutally fucked through his release.

Through the haze of pleasurable aftershocks, Lucas noticed that Jace had stopped and was backing off as if he thought this was over by a long shot. He managed to weakly grab onto the werewolf's thick arm fur.

"W-wait," he said shakily. "I still...still wanna feel that knot."

Jace whimpered, nuzzling in between Lucas' shoulders as if to say, "Are you sure?"

"Please," Lucas begged.

With a gentleness that was strange compared to the feral fucking that had just occurred, Jace scooped Lucas up into his big, strong arms. He carefully laid him down on his back, letting his head and shoulders rest against the stupidly fluffy pillows.

For a moment, Lucas thought his boyfriend was making an executive decision to stop until he found Jace looming over him again. The werewolf nudged his thighs apart with his snout before situating himself between them.

Lucas chuckled. "Wanna see my fuck-face, huh?"

An impatient huff jerked Jace's chest and his ears drew back. Lucas smoothed out the attitude by reaching up and running his hands through the soft fur of Jace's head and face. A tenderness threatened to overtake the lust in Jace's golden eyes, but within moments he was rocking his arousal against Lucas' groin.

"Come on, then," Lucas said, feeling his spent cock twitch once. "Fuck me 'til you cum."

Jace obliged immediately, returning to Lucas' raw heat in one quick movement that tore groans from each of them.

Lucas looked to where they connected and his eyes widened. In this new position, he could see his abdomen distending slightly, full of Jace's stiff rod. He placed a shaky hand to it, feeling the back-and-forth movement under his skin.

"H-holy shit, Jace," he gasped. His head fell back into the pillows as the revelation spurred his boyfriend back to his insane, deep plowing. The thrusts were becoming less and less coordinated. Not long now.

Lucas was way too oversensitive from cumming, but he didn't care. It still felt way too damn good for him to give up. He needed to be knotted, to be flooded with cum, to be bred. Fuck.

It felt like the pleasure was driving Lucas mad. The rest of his body was almost numb, his brain only focusing on the sensation of being stuffed full over and over. The only thing that mattered at that moment was Jace's dick. All he had to do was be a limp, pliant fuck-hole—just a werewolf's cock-sleeve.

Jace impossibly sped up, and Lucas became a high-pitched moaning mess. His eyes rolled as his mouth gaped, drool flowing out the corners. The knot was fully formed, slightly stretching the rim of his ass with each thrust, but not entering. Close. So close. He couldn't help the tears of pleasure that sprung to his eyes and ran down his face.

A long, rough growl rumbled through Jace's chest, and as he gave one last hard thrust, the knot popped in. At the exact same moment, Lucas' second orgasm slammed into him like a cinder block. His back arched and every muscle seemed to lock him in place as he violently shook. He could scarcely hear his own wailing moans and Jace's snarls over his heart pounding in his ears.

His limp cock twitched pathetically through it, not managing more than a few drops. It was nothing compared to Jace's which pulsed rapidly inside of him, pumping load after load. His boyfriend's hips jerked forward with each throb as if attempting to drive deeper and make sure every inch of his walls were painted white.

As the explosion of pleasure began to subside, Lucas devolved into quiet, hoarse whimpers. He breathed heavily, stroking Jace's back as the werewolf continued to convulse and unload.

Jace had collapsed onto Lucas, propped up slightly on his elbows so as not to smother him with his weight. Their chests still heaved against each other, drawing in their mingled musky scents.

Lucas groaned at the continuing flood inside him—Jace was still cumming. Holding his boyfriend through his release, he actually blacked out.

He came to probably only a few moments later. Jace had rearranged them so they were both laying on their sides, chest to chest. They were still connected. Curious, he reached between them to feel his stomach, shivering as he felt a small, but significant bulge there. Full of cum. Maybe once the knot had deflated, he would be able to push it all out and have Jace lap it up. He had to suppress a moan at the thought.

For the time being, he buried his face in the wall of fur in front of him. Jace's tree trunk of an arm snaked up to pull him closer and he felt hot breath ghosting through his hair.

Lucas smiled—exhausted, but satisfied. "Same time next month, then?"

TRAINING HIS ASS

This is the first time I was gonna hit the new gym in my neighborhood. I'm not going there to pile up muscle or anything of that sort. When it comes to my body, I'm mostly confident in my skinny frame. My height is average at 5'9.

Basically I'm going to clear my head. I'm a 20 year old down on his luck. School is a mess, and I've struggled to build meaningful relationships. So while others are probably there to get their dream body. To be as muscular as The Rock or John Cena, I'm there to vent my anger and frustration for two hours.

I carry nothing but a black tote bag. My attire is a blue pair of joggers, a silk t-shirt that fits more on the beach and the only pair of sneakers I have. A pair of sneakers that I swore to use on special events only. I hear a sound behind and see a woman carrying a red Nike gym bag on her shoulders. She's brown skinned, jacked from head to toe and much taller than me. She's probably over 6ft tall.

Once she notices I'm oogling at her, she waves and I turn my head forward. I'm naturally shy but this made my cheeks heat up. I plug my earphones and run towards the gym, already feeling embarrassed. I'm clueless as I reach there. Nobody tells me how to operate the machines. Quickly, I jump on the stationary bike and pedal my embarrassment away as she walks in.

The gym is filled with muscular hot dudes that trigger the bisexual side of me but once she walks in, my eyes go to her first and foremost. I gulp and my breathing speeds as she approaches me. I remind myself to act cool and put on an unbelieving poker face.

"Hey, you're new here?" She asks and I nod. She grins. This makes me nervous. "Of course. That was obvious. You're not supposed to start with this, silly."

Now I want to bury my face in the stand. She's changed from her jacket to a pink sports bra that shows her pointed nipples while revealing her glorious abs and biceps for all to see. Her biker shorts show her curves fully.

"Looks like you need a trainer," she says. "I'm Alexa. I can do that for you and for this first time, I'll do it for free. Are you down?" I silently nod again while freaking out inside. "Okay, youngin. Hop on the treadmill for 20 minutes. After every five minutes increase the speed by two."

Without hesitation, I hop off the bike and on the treadmill. She supervises me and corrects a lot of my errors. After that, she hands me two 10kg dumbbells and asks me to lift. When I smile smugly at the ease, she replaces them with 30kg ones and my elbows nearly give out. I drop them hard on the floor as she attends to me.

"Maybe we should focus on some stretching instead. Yoga poses too." She hurries and grabs a mat, spreading them outside. "Now raise your arms and stretch. After that, lie on your back and raise your legs up to touch your hand up. Let's see how you do these two."

I do as she says, starting by stretching out my body and then raising my legs in the air. She coughs, telling me to lift both legs up. I struggle with it but she eases me down, making my legstouch the back of my head. She touches my joggers and fondles my crotch. I gasp and break the position but she shakes her head.

"You'll need to try that again. Stand up and face me with your back." I nod without thinking and she proceeds to stretch out my arms and my back, cracking all the stiff bones. I moan as she delicately massages my standing body. "That's nice, I know this will make you feel better."

"It sure does."

"Good boy." She lets go of me and pushes me to the floor as the eyes of the others turn to us. "Ignore them and arch your back then stretch your hands forward." I do that and she slowly walks to my front. "Make sure your face touches the floor." She then goes behind me and spreads my legs, all while I breathe faster. This gets me hard. I gulp.

Hope she doesn't see her.

"What do we have here?" She rubs her hands all over my back down to my ass. I raise my back but she pushes it down and spanks my ass. The sound echoes round the gym and I want to melt under the shame. She leans closer, grinding her hips on my ass and whispers in my ears. "Nervous, baby?" I nod and she giggles. "Let's go to my personal training room. I'll give you proper training."

***

"Don't be shy, bend that ass over," she says, holding my shoulder from behind. I placed my hand on the table but she slapped my ass. "Stretch properly, touch those damn toes for me."

"Yes, Alexa."

"It's yes coach to you." I do as she says and she pulls down my pants, slowly giving little spanks while I stay in that position. "Don't get up. I want your fingertips on those toes." Once my underwear was off, she picked up a bottle of oil. "How do you come to a gym without oil, you're so unprepared."

"Sorry."

"Why are you sorry?" She laughs and rubs the oil all over my ass. "Make sure you don't shake, baby. I want us to have some fun." I moan as I feel something swirling around my ass. I gasp and clutch my toes, trying my possible best not to shake. My body vibrates as I feel a penetration. Now I start to softly shout. Her finger is inside me and she does it at full speed. As I shake around, I break position and shake. She gives me a strong slap on my ass. "What did I tell you?"

"I'm sorry coach." I whimper and she tuts. "Of course you did." She gets up as I now bend over the table in front of me. "Lie down on your back." I do as commanded and she pulls a chair to sit. "Raise your legs to touch your hand just as I taught you. And this time, don't drop your leg."

"Yes coach."

She slowly uses her tongue to swirl around my asshole while stroking my cock. I exhale. "Don't you dare drop those legs," she says and proceeds to finger me while I scream and she laughs. Out of nowhere, she plunges her mouth over my penis, bobbing it all the way to the bottom. I roll my eyes backwards. All my legs were shaking as she deepthroated me and I screamed. "Do you want me to shut you up?" She asks and I shake my head. This makes her chuckle. Her fingering and sucking continues and all through this I'm struggling for my life to hold form.

"Okay baby." She softly taps my ass. I stand and she spreads a mat on the floor then asks me to lie on it. As I lie, she puts her pussy on my face and fondles my dick in 69 position. "Eat me out like you mean it baby." I nod as we simultaneously give each other head. It's been a long while since I did this. She twerked on my face as I continued trying to lick her cunt. She on the other hand stroked me, went all the way to licking the balls before sucking yet again. She did it like an expert and it felt better than how I imagined while watching porn.

"Enough." She moaned out and stood. "Stay like that. I need to get some tools." I lay there until I felt oil once again on my ass. Before I could ask. I felt something small going to my anus. It was a butt plug. She used it to loosed me up and as she drilled me with the plug, she stretched and took my shirt off then kissed me from forehead to neck down to my sensitive nipples. I moaned from the stimulation in all places and felt like I was going to melt honestly.

"Do you like that?" She asks and I hum. She lets out a sweet giggle. "I'm getting you ready for the big one, baby." She lifts a strapon with a dildo close to 7 inches in silicone jet black. I gasp with the plug still in me. After a while, she takes the plug out and flips me on all fours. She kneels in front of Mr and places the strap in my front. This is actually gonna happen. "Stick your tongue out." I do as told and she taps my tongue with it before putting it down my throat. I choke and gag while she rubs the back of my head. "Good boy, suck my dick like that."

I nod and continue sucking it, licking the head and the balls till she forces it down my throat again. I spit on the dick and she smiles at me. "Lift your head. I wanna see those pretty eyes while you suck." I do as such. She's still dressed in the sports bra with the pants now flung away. She packed her flowing hair as I drooled on the floor. She slapped my face first with her palm and then with the strap.

After that, she kisses my forehead then goes behind me. She fondles my ass and after briefly rimming me again, she holds the cheeks tightly. "Breathe in." I feel the head going in me and my eyes pop. "Breathe out." She slowly starts to pick up the pace, going deeper and deeper. I feel the dick in my stomach. I scream, clawing the mat while she fondles my body and hammers into me. As she slows down, I begin to push back into her. I bounce back on her dick and she relishes in it.

"What a good boy. Such a good boy," she moans as I throw my ass back even twerking while I'm at it. I giggle once it fits in. It no longer hurts, now it feels like multiple orgasms are happening all at once. "Woohoo." She spanks me as I pick up my speed. "If you want to bounce so much then why don't you come on top."

I nod and climb on her, facing her directly then start going up and down all over her sock all while screaming. I reach down to touch and suck her tits. She holds my head and raises her hips to plunge her dick into me, making me moan and scream from on top of her. She silenced me with a kiss and I gole her chest, twerking like a damn strip dancer.

"Okay turn around." She reverses me and I face her with my ass. Before I start bouncing, she holds my dick and strokes it while I ride. She plunges her hips into me faster and faster while I scream. Tears water in my ears. She keeps laughing and taunting. "Awww baby. I'm sure you want me to do more of this to you, don't you?"

"Yes." I whimper as I start to feel something ready to blow. It's not just my dick but from my ass. She beeps the speed up once the precum leaves the tip. The drilling continues.

"Cum for me darling." She raises her hips as my eyes roll backward. I hold her shoulders and look up. This feels like it's too much and I can't take it. I scream as I explode in my dick and my prostate. She pushes me off her dick and onto the mat. I lay there, nearly unconscious. What a day.

She kneels beside me and kisses my cheek. "Take as much rest as you need. When you're ready, shower and drink a bullet. We still got training to do."

I nod. It was FUCKING worth it.